Sophia's Search: A Hope for Joy
Book Two of the Adven Trilogy
By Kathleen Bird

To Gage, who reminds me every day to look for the joy in reality that
God promises

"Find rest, O my soul, in God alone; my hope comes from him.
He alone is my rock and my salvation; he is my fortress, I will not be
shaken."
Psalm 62:5-6

To Sue,

Kathleen
Uird

Philippians 3:14

Acknowledgements:

Thank you to my parents and my sister who, along with my husband, always encouraged me to finish this book. Without your support it would have remained an unfinished draft on my computer. I'm so blessed that God has given me such a great support team!

Second, I would like to say thank you to Arcane Book Covers for their amazing cover design! Thanks for putting up with my questions and letting me be part of that process to create something beautiful together.

Thank you to my readers, who told me I could actually write! Thank you for falling in love with the story of Katherine and her family and for continuing to ask for the next installment of her story. Particular thanks to Miss May, whose faithful questions about when the next book would come never wavered, even after all these years.

Thank you to my friends and the rest of my family, who have loved on me and inspired me over the years. You have encouraged me in ways you could never know; and I thank you for all that you do for me and those that you encounter wherever you may be in the world.

A special thank you to Mrs. Slater, who was one of the first people to tell me I had talent. Katherine's story began in your classroom…and I'm so blessed to continue to have your encouraging presence in my life. My desire to be a writer may not have started with you, but it blossomed into reality because you were my teacher.

And last, but not least, thank you to the God who never gives up on people, but waits patiently on them to hear His voice and respond to His call. Thank you for giving me the opportunity to tell this story; and thank you for making my childhood dream a reality.

Chapter One

The sound of swordplay echoed across the courtyard. All around the combatants were the signs of spring in full bloom. Flowers covered the trees, preparing to bear fruit in the summertime. New vines were covering the sides of the castle walls. Within the castle, the sounds of children playing were heard.

In the midst of this, two opponents fought in the courtyard. Their swords clashed against each other with the resounding ring of metal on metal. Sweat poured down both faces; they'd been at it over an hour. Round and round, back and forth, first one on top and then the other. It seemed a never-ending cycle of battle.

Swish.

A sword passed through the air as the person it was aimed at moved aside. The momentum of the swing almost carried the attacker to the ground, but she recovered.

The knight dodged another blow from the now frustrated girl. "Focus!"

Another swing avoided by a quick dodge was the response. "You aren't focusing!"

This time he threw up his shield in an effort to protect from the forward thrust.

"Better, but don't let your anger get the best of you."

A pause as the girl breathed. She grunted and swung again. The older knight quickly relieved her of her sword and pushed her to the ground with his shield. She'd dropped hers early on in the fight. Before she could stop it, the sword was pointing at her neck; and she was breathing hard, lying on her back in the dirt.

"Think. Don't fight with emotion. Fight with your brain."

With that, he sheathed his sword and offered a hand to help the girl up. She grudgingly accepted, stood to her feet, and dusted herself off. There were streaks of mud all over her dress. The material was thicker, supposedly to offer some kind of protection in battle when obviously a thinner summer dress would never do. Her opinion was that it only slowed her down.

"I'm never going to get it right, Adam. You've been beating me since I was five years old. Have I ever won?"

A smile answered her complaint. "Once." He handed her the discarded sword.

She sheathed it and groaned. "You let me win that time."

"I was tired of your complaining."

"Certainly didn't stop you today."

"Would you command me to let you win, Your Majesty?"

A groan escaped her lips. She rolled her eyes in her typical fashion and started walking away. Princess Sophia would never abuse her power that way.

Honestly, she enjoyed sparring with Adam, her tutor for her whole life. He'd been defeating her with the same trick for thirteen years, ever since she'd first learned to hold a sword. It was a mean trick to play on a five-year-old with a wooden sword, but she still fell for it. Someday she was sure it would be her downfall. Not that she'd ever needed to fight for her life before.

No, as she climbed the steps to her bedroom, she knew that the skills she was learning weren't exactly useful right now. Peace had reigned in the kingdom since the day she was born. At least that's what her mother told her. Sophia believed it. Perhaps it was why it never bothered her that she wasn't as good at sword fighting as a princess probably should be. Why should it? She'd probably live her whole life in this castle and never have to draw her sword against someone else, outside of her lessons with Adam.

She rifled through her dresser, trying to find a dress to wear. It wasn't hot outside, but it wasn't cold. She was sweating from the fight. She wished she had time to bathe in the cool stream behind the castle. Her mother would be horrified that she was even thinking it. Helen and Sophia had been caught more than once playing in that very same stream when they were supposed to be studying. However, to two young girls swimming in the stream was much more enjoyable than studying to be princesses, someday queens.

Finally, she found an appropriate dress, threw it on, and rushed back down the stairs to the dining hall. Her mother and father were already seated at the head of the table. There was an empty place to the right of her mother for Sophia and another empty place to the right of her father for...

"Excuse me!" A shove accompanied the command. A young boy, well at least he seemed young to Sophia, rushed to the second empty place. His bright brown eyes lit up, and he laughed once he was seated. "Late again, Sis?"

She groaned and walked in a more appropriate manner to her own chair. Solomon may be sixteen, but he acted like he was ten. A more mischievous lad would not be found in all the kingdom. Even now, he fidgeted in his chair, eagerly awaiting his sister's response to his antics.

"You cheated."

He grinned. "I merely made a way where there was no way. You really shouldn't stand in the middle of the doorway. Anyone might come running through."

Before Sophia could make a smart remark, her father held up his hand for silence. It was time to pray to thank God for their food. She loved to hear her father pray. Every time she heard his voice talking to God, it made her heart soar. She was so proud of her father! Sometimes she wondered if he wasn't overwhelmed by the running of two kingdoms, Suffrom and Adven. He always said that God gave him the strength he needed, but Sophia thought he was looking a little more tired of late.

"God, thank you for what you have given us. You have blessed us more greatly than we could ever imagine. Thank you for the peace we have been able to enjoy these eighteen years. Thank you for the joy you have given us. Thank you for the blessings of family, friendship, and love." At this point in the prayer, he squeezed his wife's hand. Sophia smiled. "Bless what is before us today. Thank you for the opportunity to enjoy it. Amen."

When the prayer was over, everyone began eating. Sophia always enjoyed these precious moments with her family. Yes, they were sitting at a table with at least fifty other people, sometimes more, but it was still her time with her family.

"Mother?"

Queen Katherine looked away from her husband for a moment and turned to Sophia. This was her child. The apple of her eye. She looked exactly like her father. Long brown hair was flying around her face loosely. Just enough was pulled away from her face to keep it out of her eyes. Her eyes. They were like brilliant brown orbs that glowed from the joy in her heart. Ever since she was a young child, every morning was a joyful morning. Every little thing made her laugh. God had blessed her with an overwhelming abundance of laughter.

"Mother?"

Sophia's persistence interrupted her reverie. "Yes?"

"May Helen and I go for a ride this afternoon?"

"Don't you both have lessons to attend to?"

"I'm sure Eli wouldn't mind, would he, Father?"

The King turned to his daughter with a smile on his face. It never ceased to amaze him how she brought him into her arguments. How was he supposed to know the answer? "Wouldn't mind what?"

Katherine rolled her eyes. Michael tried not to laugh. Both women in his life rolled their eyes. Was that true of all women?

Sophia pushed ahead regardless of her mother's opinion. "Helen and I would like to go for a ride this afternoon." She lowered her voice to almost a whisper. "Instead of having our lessons?"

"And you think Eli wouldn't mind that?"

"Not if you gave us permission…" She blinked rapidly. It was her attempt to persuade him without words. It always worked.

"I suppose missing one day of lessons won't hurt."

There were her eyes again! They lit up like fireflies in the summertime. "Thank you, Father!" She jumped up from the table and gave him a hug. Before he and Katherine could do anything else, she was running out of the room.

Solomon watched her as he continued to eat. "A little excited, isn't she?" He placed another scoop of food on his plate before continuing. "What could be so exciting about a ride?"

Michael smiled at his wife. "I think it's exciting, simply because it can be."

Sophia went running through the castle hallways straight to where she knew Helen would be. With her mother. Queen Ralyn's room was on the upper floor, with a balcony overlooking the garden. She loved the garden. It was perhaps the only thing she truly enjoyed. Helen had tried over and over to get her to smile. It didn't seem possible. Ever since the death of her husband, Ralyn had been withdrawn. Her faith had withered and become stagnant. Nothing seemed to pierce the blackness of her grief. Eighteen years of depression weighed on her heavily. Many years had passed since Helen had had joy in her life. Her mother's depression weighed on her mind as well.

When Sophia opened the door, she saw Helen sitting on the bed reading a book. Her dark eyes sparkled with delight at the interruption. "Sophia? What's all the excitement about?"

"Father has given his consent for us to go riding this afternoon."

Helen laughed a little. "Why is this so exciting?"

The eyes rolled. "Don't you see? We've been trapped inside doing nothing but lessons all winter. This is a chance to go outside the castle walls for once! This is a chance for freedom, even if it's for one afternoon."

"Freedom?" Helen's bitter laugh sounded hollow in the semi-empty room. "True freedom is only found far from here."

Sophia bounced on her toes. This kind of comment was expected. Helen could sometimes be just as bitter as her mother.

With a yawn and a stretch, Helen rose from the bed. She lazily turned her head toward the balcony where her mother was. "Mother, I'm going out."

There was no response. Helen shrugged and walked to the door. Sophia followed right behind. That kind of thing was expected.

The galloping of horses' hooves. It was a thing that never ceased to amaze Sophia. Sometimes she thought that she had been born riding a horse. That was how natural it felt to be sitting in the saddle with the countryside passing beneath her dangling feet. The wind was blowing her hair out of her face. The sun shone brightly all around her. Even Helen's dark mood had not been able to dismay her today. The feeling of freedom was so invigorating. Even her failed lesson this morning was far away. Nothing could touch her, not while she was here on her horse.

Behind her, Helen rode in silence. What went on half the time in her mind, Sophia didn't know. She constantly seemed to be in a cloud of darkness. When they were children, they played and laughed. They had joy in their lives. But as they grew up, somehow the joy that remained in Sophia left Helen. Somewhere along the way, Helen changed. Just when that happened, she never could figure out.

They were not too far from the castle when the two girls looked back to see another figure riding after them. Even from far away, they knew who he was.

"Edwin. Father sent Edwin out to ride with us."

Helen nodded as they waited for the fast approaching rider. It was indeed Edwin. He sat high in his seat, with his head held high. He looked more like a man than a disheveled boy now, although Adam often teased him for the three red hairs he called a beard. One hand rested on his sword while his eyes darted around, looking for enemy activity. Once, when she was too young to know better, Sophia had asked him why he did that. Edwin's response to her had been a little more than a ten-year-old could handle. The thought of enemies attacking her and carrying her off to some unknown place terrified her. She had nightmares for weeks afterward. Michael and Katherine had been angry, but they quickly forgave Edwin.

Now, he rode quickly after them. When he reached them, he pulled on the reigns and smiled. "Your Father sent me, Sophia. He wanted to make sure you girls weren't out too far from the castle."

"Is this too far?"

"It's coming close, but you may ride out a little further if you stay with me."

"Of course." The voice was Helen's and dripped with sarcasm.

Edwin glanced sideways at Helen. She sat slightly behind Sophia, and her piercing dark eyes glared at their guide.

"What did you say?" His eyes flashed. It may have been eighteen years since he last fought a war, but he was still a knight. He wouldn't stand for insolence.

Helen glared back but refused to answer. Sophia prayed that God would intervene. She didn't want a fight. It was too beautiful a day.

Lucky for her, Edwin dropped the matter, clicked his tongue to his horse, and started off again. Sophia followed him. She turned to glance at Helen, who was still sitting on her horse glaring. A moment later and she was following, slowly, but following.

"Why did you do that?"

"Do what?"

Sophia groaned and sprawled on her bed. Sometimes her cousin drove her up the wall. "Why were you so rude to Edwin?"

A glare was, for a moment, her only response. When it became clear Sophia wasn't going to drop the subject, Helen sighed and said, "Don't you ever get tired of them following you?"

"We're princesses. Edwin is only there to protect us."

"Protect us from what?" Helen's anger surprised her cousin. Where was all this coming from? Her eyes flashed, and she almost shook with the strength of her wrath. She spun away from Sophia and paced the opposite side of the room. Her feet made no sound on the floor, except for the soft swishing of her dress. However, the anger almost felt like a third person standing in the room, ready to strike.

Helen took a breath and continued her tirade. "There has been peace in this kingdom as far back as I can remember! Why would it ever be different? No. Our parents are not afraid of enemies stealing us away." She paused and turned back to face her cousin. Now her eyes sparkled with a new light that was rather frightening. "Here is the truth, my dear cousin. They are afraid of our imaginations. They are afraid we will run away ourselves, because we want one thing: freedom."

"Why would I run away? Why would you?" Sophia leapt up from the bed and threw open the balcony to her right. "Do you see this?" She motioned to the gardens and the castle walls beyond. "This is our life! This is where we are meant to be! God..."

"Don't speak of God!" Helen's vehemence was frightening. She looked like she could start a fight if she really wanted to. "What has God ever done for me?"

Sophia did not respond. She was surprised. She knew that Helen was bitter, but she never knew that she had abandoned her faith. What could she say? There was nothing that would dissuade her cousin from her anger at God.

Breakfast the next day was quiet. There were only four seated at the table: Michael, Katherine, Sophia, and Solomon. No one spoke. Even Solomon refrained from telling any of his infamous jokes. One bite of food followed another, yet still no one spoke. Sophia tried to calm her nerves, but they refused to be quiet. Her stomach rolled, and she felt like crying.

"It wasn't my fault."

Michael and Katherine looked up from their plates without a word. Their eyes looked at her without expression.

"I didn't mean for Edwin's feelings to get hurt."

"Edwin will be fine." Katherine's voice was calm, yet still without expression.

"Still, I didn't mean..."

"We know." Michael smiled at her. "You're not in trouble. But we are concerned."

Solomon munched his food loudly, swallowing with a loud hiccup. His sister glared at him. He merely shrugged and went back to eating. Sophia tried to ignore him as she asked, "Concerned about what?"

It was Katherine's turn to respond, but she took her time. Glancing at her husband, she took a deep breath before continuing. "About Helen."

"What about her?"

Another pause. "How is she?"

Sophia shoved another bite of food in her mouth in order to delay her answer. "Well, I suppose. Why?"

Michael put one hand on his wife's to calm her. Clearly her mother was a little overly ambitious to get the problem solved. Her father spoke calmly and directly. "What did she say to you after the two of you got back?"

Sophia paused and almost choked on her food. "Excuse me?"

Before Michael could respond, Sophia was on her feet. "Why does it matter? Can't two cousins talk in the privacy of their rooms? Must you know everything we say, everything we do, everything we secretly wish for?" Her voice rose in both pitch and volume with every word.

Before Michael or Katherine could say anything, Sophia was venting again. "We're royalty, princesses; but what does that mean? We can't do anything without an escort, a guard. We…"

"Sophia."

She stopped long enough to look into her parents' eyes. They were clearly concerned. The King tried to keep his voice even. "Do you really believe all that?"

She stuttered and finally settled for silence.

Her father looked her straight in the eyes and finished his thought. "Or is that just Helen talking?"

Sophia turned bright red, pushed her plate away, and stormed out of the dining hall.

Chapter Two

"She's mad."

"That's a bit of an understatement, Michael."

Katherine's tone was tired, exhausted from worry about their oldest daughter. "She hasn't spoken to us for two days."

"And Helen?"

Katherine shook her head.

The King sat down on the edge of the bed. The room was not as tiny as it had been eighteen years ago. They had more furniture than just a wardrobe and a chair. Actually, the room was quite spacious. They still had a window that faced out toward the rolling hills of Adven. They could even see the beginning of the village that had formed about ten years ago just up the road from the castle. It was growing at a fast pace with new people arriving almost every day. That little village was like a picture of Adven as a whole. The kingdom prospered, and the people flourished. Everyone was happy. Except the princesses apparently.

Michael shook his head again. "Why is she acting like this all of a sudden?" He ran his hand through his hair and stroked his beard. His wife knew that meant he was troubled.

"Helen. You said it yourself. Somehow Helen's bitterness finally got through to her." Katherine sighed. "That child needs the hope for a better tomorrow that Ralyn wouldn't give her."

"God will take care of her, if she would just let Him."

"I know." Katherine smiled as she looked at him. Her eyes sparkled like they did on their wedding day. "But, it's nice to hear you tell me again."

He smiled and got up off the bed. Gently, he took her hands in his and kissed her forehead. They both stood for a moment, simply enjoying the other's presence. The sun shone in through their window and alighted on the sword hanging over the fireplace. The couple noticed; and with a smile, Katherine removed the sword from where it hung.

Yes, this was her sword hanging on the mantel in their bedroom. The kingdom had been at peace for so long that no one but the knights needed to keep their swords with them. She had retired hers to this place of honor. It had received enough attention in the days following the war to become something of a legend, along with its bearer. Queen Katherine was respected and loved by all, the true bloodline of Adven. She was the pride and joy of the kingdom, as she was to her husband.

With an almost silent sound of the sword against the sheath, she drew the sword. Immediately the blade blazed with light and filled the room. It seemed like the presence of God was filling the room as the light spread to all the dark corners. All fears and worries flew away while the couple stood in that wonderful presence. After a moment, Katherine sheathed the sword; and the light dissolved back into the blade. She hung it back on its hook and turned to Michael.

"I just wanted to see if it still did it."

"Of course," he said as he smiled. "It will always shine with the love that you have for both God and the people around you."

She smiled as she pondered the words written on the sword. They were a commandment for husband and wife to love each other, but also to love God unconditionally. It was Katherine and Michael's secret code to tell each other of their love.

The moment was broken when they heard a yell from out in the hallway. It sounded like Helen.

"Stay out of my room! What right have you to be in here?" Helen's voice carried throughout the castle as Michael and Katherine rushed down the hallway to see the recipient of her wrath. Solomon lay on the floor, as though he had literally been thrown from the room. His normally happy face was furrowed with a mixture of frustration and anger.

"I was simply looking for Sophia! You didn't answer when I knocked."

"So, you thought you would come in without an invitation?"

"I didn't know I needed one."

"Of course you didn't."

Solomon stood and dusted himself off. He glared at Helen eye to eye. Even though he was two years her junior, he would soon pass her height. "I beg your pardon."

She didn't answer but instead returned his glare. Her eyes were bright with the anger that so often lit them of late. When she did speak, it came in hard even tones. "Don't let it happen again."

With that, she slammed her door in his face, leaving a frustrated Solomon to answer his parents' questions. Michael and Katherine gave him a moment to regain his focus before they asked him anything.

Michael was the first to speak. "Why were you looking for Sophia?"

Solomon turned from the closed door to face his father. "I simply wanted to borrow one of her books. She was not in her room, so I thought she might be with Helen."

"Next time just wait until dinner to ask her." Katherine smiled at her son. Sometimes simple solutions escaped him.

Michael waved his hand down the hallway. "Don't you have lessons to attend to? I'm sure Eli is waiting for you."

Solomon gave a short bow and turned to run down the hallway towards the library.

Michael and Katherine looked at each other for a moment before stepping forward to knock on Helen's door.

"I thought I told you to get out!" Helen's anger came before her as she flung the door back open. Her eyes were still filled with frustration until she realized who was standing in her doorway. As soon as she recognized the King and Queen, she remembered her manners and offered a formal bow. "My apologies, Your Majesties. I thought…"

"We know who you thought was out here," Katherine smiled in an attempt to dispel the tension in the air. "He has been properly scolded and sent to his lessons in the library for his troubles."

Helen simply nodded and looked eager to retreat back into her bedroom.

Michael locked eyes with her to evaluate the best way to proceed. After a short moment of thought, he turned to his wife and spoke. "I'm going to check on a few things, Katherine. I will talk to you later." He kissed her on her cheek, said a quick good-bye to Helen, and walked on down the hallway.

It was then just Katherine and Helen. The two looked at each other, sizing each other up. The Queen groaned. It had never been this hard with Sophia.

"Helen, may I come in for just a moment?"

The young woman stepped out of the doorway to allow her aunt inside. Inside, the room was dark as a cloud passed over the sun. About half of the windows were covered, and the other half open. On one wall stood an elegant bookshelf filled with a variety of books, ranging from histories of Suffrom to the fairytales that Eli used to make up for the girls when they were younger. Her bed was unmade, and there were clothes thrown on the floor in little piles.

"Finished checking up on my room? It's not the cleanest this week. Is that why you're upset?"

"Helen, I'm not here to check up on you. I'm not mad at you. I just wanted to talk to you. Is that okay?"

"I suppose so." And with that, she flopped down on her bed, arms sprawling across the whole mattress and head thrown back against the pillows while staring at the ceiling. "Go ahead and talk, Aunt Katherine."

"Just a moment ago, you called me Your Majesty. Why the change?"

Helen rolled her eyes. "You said you wanted to talk to me. Most queens don't "talk" to the princesses of neighboring countries."

Katherine settled herself on the edge of the bed, gingerly pushing aside a few discarded dresses. "I'm just concerned about you."

"No need to be concerned. I'm just fine."

"Are you sure? You seemed pretty upset at Edwin the other day and at Solomon just now…"

Helen sat up and glared icily at her aunt. "Look, they have no right to invade my privacy. I can do whatever I like."

"We have certain rules in place to protect you when it comes to traveling. You and Sophia are both required to be accompanied by a knight when you ride out beyond a certain point..."

"Why?"

"For your own safety..."

"What could possibly hurt us out there?" Helen stood up and angrily marched to the window. "The war is over, Aunt Katherine. There is no enemy hiding in the shadows. Yet, we still remain here. Trapped behind these walls and forced to live our daily lives with no knowledge of what's going on in the world around us!"

"We are only trying to protect you girls."

Helen motioned toward the window. "There is so much to see out there! Why won't you let us find out for ourselves?"

"Maybe when you're older..."

"We're eighteen years old! My mother was married by that time!"

"You're not your mother."

"Right. I don't have a dead husband and a child to take care of."

Katherine's jaw dropped at Helen's statement. There was nothing she could think of to say. Instead, she rose quietly from the bed and walked to the door. Before she left, she turned around and said, "I'm sorry you feel that way, Helen. We'll have to continue this discussion at another time."

She stepped into the hallway and turned to close the door. Before she could grasp the door handle, Helen marched over and slammed it in her face. Katherine heard sobbing as she walked away.

Knock. Knock. Knock.

"Go away. I don't want to see anyone."

The door creaked open anyway. Sophia gently poked her head through the partially open doorway and scanned the room. When nothing was thrown at her, she walked the rest of the way in the room. "Helen?"

"I said go away."

"I'm not going away. I brought you something to eat. You missed dinner."

"I'm not hungry."

Sophia sat the tray she was carrying on a side table and then moved to the bed. Helen lay with her face buried in her pillow. Her clothes were ruffled, and she looked like she hadn't moved from her face down position in some time. "What do you want, Sophia?" Her voice seemed tired.

"I want to know what is wrong with you. Mother mentioned that she tried to talk to you this afternoon, and you practically threw her out! What is going on, Helen?"

She sat up on the bed and turned her tear-streaked face to her cousin. "It's never going to change." She wiped a new tear trail from her cheek.

"What's never going to change?"

"Our parents. This life. It's like I said before, we're never going to find freedom inside this place. Real living is outside these walls."

"I'm perfectly happy right where I am. Why can't you be happy, Helen?"

She glared at Sophia. "Why should I be? I am nothing but a charity case in your parent's home. There is nothing here for me. But, out there…" She got off the bed and threw open the window. "Just look at the world, Sophia! There is so much to see and to do. I've never even been to Suffrom, and I'm supposed to rule there someday!"

"I'm sure you'll get there eventually." Sophia's disinterested tone reflected her attitude. This type of conversation was happening more and more frequently, but eventually Helen tired of it and discussed something else. This time would be no different.

But it was. Helen ran from the window, grabbed Sophia's hands, and sat next to her on the bed. "Don't you ever wonder what would happen if we got away for just a little bit. A year or so on our own would do us good, don't you think?"

"What are you talking about?"

"Leaving this place! Getting away."

Sophia was so shocked it took her a moment to process the statement. "You can't really mean that!"

"But I do! I'm tired of this, Sophia. I'm leaving. Tonight. You are more than welcome to come with me, but either way I am leaving."

Solomon was reading the book finally acquired from his sister and not really paying attention as he walked down the hallway. Therefore, he was completely taken by surprised when the aforementioned sister ran into him.

"Solomon!"

He paused in his reading a moment to look up at the person he'd collided with. "Sorry, Sophia. This is just really interesting." It was then he noticed the bag in her hands. "What's in there?"

"Nothing!" She tried to push past him, and an apple fell out.

He picked it up off the floor and looked at it quizzically. "Didn't get enough to eat at dinner?"

She snatched the apple from his hands and shoved it back into the bag. "Yes. I just wanted a little snack before bed. Is that a problem?"

He backed off and continued walking down the hallway. "Of course. I was just asking. Sorry to bother you."

Sophia stood watching him walk away for a minute and then raced after him. Catching him in a hug from behind, he dropped the book in an attempt to wriggle away. "I'm sorry. I shouldn't have yelled at you. Forgive me?"

Finally freeing himself, he dusted off any sister germs left on his clothes and picked up the dropped book. "Of course. Are you sure you're feeling okay?"

"Perfectly fine. I'll talk to you later, Solomon."

Without another word, she was rushing down the hall towards Helen's room. The door opened and closed quickly, and he heard whispering inside. Not particularly out of the ordinary of late. Solomon turned his attention back to his book and continued in the opposite direction.

"Mother? Father?"

"Come in, Sophia." Her father's voice sounded happy to see her, so she eagerly pushed open their bedroom door. Both were dressed for bed but were sitting talking to each other.

Michael sat on the edge of the bed itself. Katherine sat in a chair, sewing a rip in one of her dresses. Both looked pleased to see their oldest child coming in to talk to them. Her mother was the first to speak. "What is it, Sophia? Is everything alright?"

"Yes. I just wanted to apologize for the way I've been acting lately."

"Everything is already forgiven," Michael said. He smiled.

Sophia danced on her toes, unsure of how to proceed without raising suspicion. She knew what she wanted to ask, what Helen had told her to ask, but she didn't know how to go about it.

"Anything else you wanted to tell us?" her father gently prodded, seeing her hesitation.

"Well, it's really more of a question."

"Go ahead." Her mother stopped sewing to focus on Sophia.

"Um…I just wondered…I was thinking…" She took a deep breathing and plunged ahead. "I was wondering what happens when I'm old enough to take the throne."

Michael and Katherine looked at each other. It was Katherine who spoke first. "What made you wonder that?"

"I was just…wondering. That's all."

Father thought for a moment. "You would be ruler of Adven. Essentially, anything after that would be up to you."

Sophia came over and sat on the bed beside him. "I guess what I was really wondering about was…" She paused. "I really shouldn't ask." She started to get up before her father placed his hand on hers and urged her back to her seat.

"What is it?"

Her big brown eyes looked over to her mother, carefully evaluating her present mood. "I was wondering about the sword."

"The sword?" Katherine looked puzzled for a moment. "What sword?"

"Your sword. The one mounted on the wall. When I'm old enough, would that be mine also?"

Michael and Katherine looked at each other again. She spoke softly and slowly. "Well, I suppose so. If we felt you were ready."

"How would you know when I'm ready?"

They thought again. Michael said cautiously, "I guess the sword itself would show us."

Katherine set down her sewing and walked across to the sword hanging on the wall. She took it down and carefully unsheathed it. The moment her hand touched the hilt, the sword started glowing with its bright light. "The sword is blessed by the one true God. It senses the purity and love in the bearer's heart and shines with the light of God if the bearer truly believes."

"You see, Sophia," Michael continued. "if the sword shines like it does when your mother holds it, then you are more than welcome to it. We will trust that that is the time for it to be passed on to you."

Sophia started to reach for the sword, but her mother slid it back into its sheath and mounted it back on the wall. "Someday, it will be yours, but I think you'd better be getting to bed now. I know you've got a lesson with Adam tomorrow afternoon, and you'll want to be well rested."

Before she could say another word, she found herself shooed out into the hallway.

Chapter Three

"I don't feel right about this, Helen."

"You've got to, Sophia."

The two stood whispering in the hallway outside the King and Queen's bedroom. On their backs were bags containing clothes and some food, with more bags of food sitting on the ground beside them waiting to be loaded onto the horses. Helen stood with one hand on her hip, and the other holding a dying candle. The moon was hidden by a cloud, so no light was shining in the castle. The light shed by her candle was just barely enough to see Sophia's nervous expression.

"But they didn't give it to me."

"They said someday it'd be yours, right?"

"Yes, but…"

"So that someday is today! Go in there and get the sword. I'm getting one from the armory and meeting you with the horses. You had better have that sword, Sophia."

With that, she marched off with a bag of food in her free hand. As the candlelight trickled away, Sophia found herself shivering in the darkness.

"It's simple. Just open the door, take it off the wall, and walk back out."

The door didn't even creak as she opened it. Walking on tiptoes, she crept into the room and walked to where she knew the sword was hanging. Guilt rushed through her as she reached up to take the sword. Carefully, she removed it and held the sword by its sheath. Now, unsure of what to do, she ran her hand along the length of the sheath until she reached the hilt. Pausing before she touched it, she thought and made her decision.

Gently, she grasped the hilt and drew the sword. Bright light filled the room, and fear shot through her. The light filled every part of the room and lit up even the dark corners. Her hand shook, and she grabbed the sword with both hands. Fumbling, and frightened the light would wake up her parents, she tried to sheathe the sword.

Suddenly, the hilt became white hot and burned almost as brightly as the blade. Sophia let out a little squeak and dropped the sword on the ground. The light instantly faded.

Fear shot through her, but as she reached down to pick the sword up and put it away, it didn't light up, nor did it burn her hand. Afraid of what she had done and wracked with guilt, she buckled the sword to the belt already on her waist and ran out of the room, closing the door behind her.

Helen was already on her horse, waiting for Sophia, when she came running down the stairs with the sword and two more bags of food. Quickly tying the bags to her own horse, she mounted with one jump and pulled in front of her cousin.

"What took you so long? I've been waiting at least five minutes."

"Nothing. Don't worry about it. Are you ready to go?"

A quick nod was her only answer.

The clouds still covered the moon as the two princesses rode their horses to the rear of the castle, still inside the walls. It was a newer addition to the ancient building, but useful for a quick escape in the dead of night. The little creek had been opened up more, and the water flowed to a secret tunnel deep beneath the castle. Michael had insisted it be built in case of an enemy attack. He said that it would provide a way out for the women and children, unbeknownst to the attackers.

Stealthily, the two girls rode their horses down the stairs. Even the sound of the horses' hooves on the cobblestone steps sounded like an alarm bell announcing their exit.

"Can't you go any faster?" Helen whispered as she nudged her horse into Sophia's. A snort from the horse in the front could be heard, while Sophia tried to urge it to a faster pace.

The lapping of the creek announced their arrival at the bottom of the entryway. Carefully trotting along the creek bed, they came to the secret doorway. It was nothing special, just a wooden door with a metal bar across it; but to the girls preparing to go through, it seemed like the portal to another world.

It was Helen who pushed her way past Sophia and dismounted to open the door. The heavy clink of the metal bar against the stone surrounding the doorway echoed throughout the empty cavern. Sophia urged her horse through the door and pulled the reigns of Helen's horse along with her. After she was through, Helen pulled the door shut behind them and they heard the metal bar fall back into place. Now, they were completely separated from the world they once knew. The only way out was forward.

"Katherine! Michael!"

The frantic voice pierced through Katherine's deep state of sleep. She blinked and opened her eyes, scanning the room for the source of the voice. Next to her, Michael was also stirring.

Just then, the door burst open and Eli came running into the room as fast as he could. "I'm sorry to wake you, but this is urgent." He bowed and waited for the royal couple to acknowledge him.

"What is it, Eli? What is so important?" Michael sat up and helped Katherine to sit up also. He rubbed his eyes and waited for the answer.

"The princesses are gone."

Instantly awake, Katherine threw aside the sheets and started reaching for her clothes. "Are you sure they aren't just out on a ride or something? Down by the creek? Hiding out in one of their bedrooms?"

Eli shook his head. "We've searched everywhere. One of the knights found this in Princess Sophia's bedroom." He handed Michael a hastily written note.

It read:

Dear Mother, Father, and Solomon,

I couldn't let her go alone.
I love you.

I promise I'll come back.

Sophia

"Michael, what can we do? Where could they be going?"
Katherine was becoming more frantic by the minute, and there was
nothing he could do about it. Rubbing his beard and holding the note
in the other hand, he read the note again, and then a third time.

"Helen. Helen told her she would run away, and Sophia
wouldn't let her go alone." He looked up and met Katherine in the
eyes. "Did Helen say anything yesterday that might give us some idea
of where they are going?"

She shook her head. "She kept talking about how she's not a
child anymore and how she wanted to see the world…" A tear slipped
down her face. "I guess she did, and I didn't take note of it. I was so
focused elsewhere…" Katherine covered her face with her hands.

Michael reached over and pulled her close. He looked at Eli.
"Send Edwin after them. That's all we can do for now."

Eli closed the door behind him on the grief-stricken parents.
Adam was standing in the hallway waiting for him. "What did they
say?"

The elderly man wrung his hands and hung his head. Sadly, he
said, "Katherine is crying. She's blaming herself." A few more tears
slipped down his cheeks. "He's trying to comfort her. He
commanded me to send Edwin after them."

"Already done," Adam said. "The boy was gone as soon as he
heard. He suspected they'd gone out the tunnel by the creek and
figured he could track them from there. How far could they have
gotten in one night?"

Eli shrugged. With his head still hanging, he started down the
hallway. "I'd best go tell Solomon. If he takes my advice, he will be
on his knees before God within the next ten minutes."

"Helen! Wait up! Slow down!"

Sophia pushed her horse to move faster, but it merely snorted at her and kept on at its present pace. Giving in, she allowed him to stop and graze. Noticing the missing sound of galloping behind her, Helen finally stopped her own horse and turned around to come back with Sophia.

"We can't stop now. I want to put as much distance as possible in between us and the castle."

"We can't keep riding at this pace! The horses need rest. We've been driving them all night." She ran a hand through her hair. "And I can't keep going like this either."

Helen sniffed. "I suppose we could stop for a little while." She dismounted and walked her horse over to where Sophia's was grazing.

Sophia dismounted and walked over to a tree to lean against while she sat. "Where are we going anyway?"

"I don't know. It doesn't really matter. Anywhere away from the castle."

"But we can't just keep riding in circles. We need to decide where we are headed. That way we know how to get home when the time comes."

"Who said anything about going back?"

Sophia just blinked. "Of course, we'll go back." She shrugged. "Someday."

Helen sat down on the grass next to her. "I don't know about that."

"How can we not? My place is at the castle. Your place is on the throne of Suffrom. You can't give that up!"

"I didn't say I'd give it up."

Sophia tried to breathe and keep her head clear. "Make sense, Helen!"

Her cousin didn't answer her. Instead she walked over to her horse and mounted. Turning his head in the direction they were headed before, she said, "Now you know," she paused to allow Sophia time to mount her own horse. "I'm never going back to the castle." She spurred her horse onward, and away from the castle.

"Any sign of them?"

"I'm afraid not, Your Majesty."

"Thanks anyway, Eli." Katherine turned her back to the doorway and continued looking out the window.

Eli didn't leave as she expected he would. Instead, he walked over to her and tried to coax her out. "Edwin will find them."

The Queen walked away from Eli and the window and began pacing before the fireplace. "There's a thousand ways they could have gone. Any number of things that could go wrong! They could be lying somewhere dying, alone, and forgotten, just like..." She bit her lip and didn't continue.

Eli knew the rest of the thought without her saying it. The pain of losing both Mother and Father had never healed completely for Katherine. Most of the time her faith kept her afloat, but times like this reminded her of the time she spent worrying about King Andrew while he was away fighting the war.

His shaking hand pressed softly on her arm. Eli certainly was not getting any younger. He had spent most of his lifetime serving his rulers, and a large part of it watching over her and her family. Wisdom for every situation came with age, and with his faith in the One True God. This was no exception.

"Katherine, Sophia knows how to take care of herself."

No response.

"Has Ralyn been told?"

A nod.

"What did she say?"

"Nothing."

Eli paused to think about that. "Nothing?"

Tears began to trickle anew down Katherine's cheeks. "She just kept staring out at the garden and said nothing. It was like she didn't even hear me."

"She's just as worried as you are."

Anger edged her voice as she said, "But she's not the one who's going to do anything about it." And then resolution. "I'm going after her myself." She turned to grab her sword and walk out the door.

"Katherine, I don't..."

She gasped, and panic filled her as she turned to rush out the door, calling Michael's name as she ran through the halls. It was then that Eli saw what she had seen.

The sword was gone.

Michael was sitting alone in the throne room, head in his hands, praying that God would bring his little girl back to him. The startled sounds of servants and loud shouting broke into his thoughts. Before he could even attempt to discern who was screaming, Katherine burst into the empty hall.

"Michael! She took it!"

"Who took what?"

"Sophia took my sword." Katherine's voice was becoming more panicked the more she had to repeat herself.

Michael stepped down from the raised dais and walked toward his wife. His walk was heavy with the weight of worry on his shoulders. Was God even listening to his prayers? Things seemed to be getting worse and worse.

Silently, he took his wife and enfolded her into his arms, trying to quiet the sobs that racked her body. Tears began to flow from his own eyes in the midst of his attempts to comfort her.

"What's going to happen to her, Michael?"

He tried to keep his voice calm and even as he replied, "I don't know, Katherine. I just don't know."

Chapter Four

"I can't go any further, Helen! We have to stop and rest!"

Sophia was disliking the "world" more and more every hour that went by. She would much rather have been sword fighting with Adam or discussing God with Eli or even talking to Solomon about the latest book he's read. Already, she missed Mother and Father. Part of missing them was guilt for leaving without saying good-bye, and another constant reminder of her guilt was the sword bumping against her side.

Finally paying attention to her cousin's request, Helen slowed her horse to a stop and hopped off. "Fine. We can stop here for the night. I think we've gotten plenty of distance between us and Edwin."

"Edwin?" Sophia questioned as she led her horse to the tiny creek next to their stopping point. There were hundreds of these little rivulets that flowed all through Adven's forests. It meant easier travel for those going from one end of the forest to the other and ready access to fresh drinking water.

Helen rolled her eyes as she led her own horse to the creek. "Who do they always send after us? They'll have sent Edwin out to track us as soon as they realized we were gone." She grinned. "But he won't have expected us to ride through the forest without stopping."

Sophia didn't respond. She held tightly to her horse's reigns to keep her hands from shaking. Only now was she beginning to realize that Helen was truly cutting ties with everyone and everything back at the castle. How was she ever going to convince her when it was time to go back home?

The two girls tied their horses to the branches of a couple trees and sat down to eat something. Neither were particularly hungry, so they settled for a few apples each. Both girls sat quietly contemplating what the repercussions might be for their actions, but quickly moved on to focus on the exciting things they might be able to see and do now that they were free from the watchful eyes of the King and Queen. In the end, it was Sophia who broke the silence.

"Helen?"

"Yes?" she said as she munched on the last bit of her third apple.

"Did you tell your mother what we were doing?"

"No. Why should I?"

"Well," Sophia paused before continuing. "Won't she be worried about you?"

Helen sighed and stared into the forest. "My mother can't even stand to look at me. It's better for both of us that I'm gone."

"That's not true!" Sophia moved closer to her cousin and put her hand on her shoulder. "She loves you!"

"Maybe she did once, but not anymore."

"But…"

"Sophia, just drop it!" Helen angrily pulled away from her cousin's gentle touch. She stood up and stalked off into the forest. Sophia didn't see her again until after she woke up the next morning.

"Ralyn."

No response came from the balcony. Katherine took it as an invitation to come in. Nothing had been moved since Helen left. Ralyn still sat in her rocking chair on the balcony overlooking the garden. It looked like she hadn't moved in years.

Moving as quietly as possible, Katherine walked up to her younger sister. Where was the smile she had so enjoyed as a child? Where was the laughter they had shared so many times? What had happened to the dreams they'd whispered as they played in the creek or eavesdropped outside the throne room, pretending to understand what went on inside? The person sitting before her now was a mere shell of the person she had been.

"Ralyn, will you speak to me?"

No response.

Katherine knelt beside the chair and put her hand on her sister's. It looked so frail and lifeless with hardly any warmth emanating from it. "Ralyn?"

"Is it true?"

"Is what true?"

Ralyn's voice was shaking from disuse. "Helen is gone?"

"I'm afraid so."

"And Sophia?"

Katherine tried to hold back the tears. "Gone too."

"Where could they be going?"

"I don't know. It all happened so quickly."

"I should have known it would happen."

That made Katherine listen closely. "Had Helen mentioned leaving?"

But Ralyn didn't hear the question. She was staring out at the garden bursting into full bloom. "God took away Evan. Now He's taken away Helen. He's taken everything I ever loved away from me."

"Don't blame this on God!" Katherine was alarmed at the things coming from her sister's mouth. When their Mother died, it was Ralyn who pushed through and found comfort in her faith. She was then able to give Katherine comfort until she found peace in her own faith. Now it sounded like her sister had given up on God completely.

"Who else can I blame it on? I didn't want Evan to fight Adven's war. I didn't want Helen to run away. It certainly isn't my fault." She looked at her sister. "I suppose it could be your fault."

"My fault!"

"Evan died fighting your war. Helen ran off with your daughter. I'm a charity case in your house." Ralyn's eyes drifted away from Katherine and glazed over as they stared at the garden. "And now I will die alone and forgotten, just like Father."

The pain in Katherine's heart was almost too much for her to bear, but she shoved it down and tried to uplift Ralyn. "Everything will work out. We'll get Helen back. Edwin has probably already found her and is on his way…"

"No!" Ralyn's emphatic answer surprised her.

"No?"

"I don't ever want to see her again. I just want to be left to die in peace."

"Ralyn!"

"Katherine," she said with an edge to her voice and a volume that hedged on shouting, "get out of my chambers and don't come back."

With no other options left at her disposal, Katherine turned and silently walked back inside, through Helen's room, and back into the hallway. The quiet click of the closing door was her only response as she pulled it shut.

The horses continued galloping at a steady pace. The two princesses rode in silence, each lost in their own thoughts. Sophia sighed, frustrated at this seemingly foolish turn of events. What was she doing out here? What did she expect to find outside the castle that could not be found inside? Already she missed Mother, Father, Eli, Edwin, Adam, and even Solomon. It took everything within her to keep from turning back around. But the thought of riding back alone was something she didn't want to have to experience. So instead, she kept following Helen, who rode tall in the saddle about twenty feet in front of her, wherever her fancy led.

The sun climbed higher and higher into the sky, making it harder to keep up the fast pace Helen so desired. But no matter what Sophia tried; Helen would not slow down. In fact, they did not stop again until the sun had fallen deep into the western horizon and the air was beginning to grow cooler. The girls collapsed onto the soft grass, taking care to tie the horses to a tree close by.

"Helen."

"Yes?"

"You've got to have some idea where we are going." It was a statement, not a question.

"No, not really."

Sophia rolled over and looked Helen squarely in the eyes. The past couple days had been long, and her nerves were wearing thin. Adventuring was not nearly as fun as she thought it'd be. "Yes, really. We need to have a direction to go so we don't ride in circles." She paused to think. "And 'away from the castle' is not a direction."

There was no immediate response from Helen. Sophia almost started talking again before she heard, "Towards Suffrom. We'll head towards Suffrom. I want to see my home." Her voice choked a little. "I want to see what might have been if..."

Sophia waited to see if Helen would say anything else. After a few minutes, "Goodnight, Sophia."

"Goodnight, Helen."

When the sun rose, they started on their journey once more. Now that Helen had finally admitted to some sort of final destination, Sophia pushed her to continue on. She figured the sooner they made it to Suffrom, the sooner they could return to Adven. Continuing south and east, they rode hard all day and stopped by a stream. They were resting and refilling their water when a sound came from across the small clearing.

"Did you hear that, Helen?" Sophia's voice was shaking, and she trembled with fear.

"Get behind those bushes!" Helen whispered fiercely and shoved her cousin behind the shrubbery.

As the girls bent down to hide from whomever was appearing through the trees, Helen drew her sword from its sheath. Sophia simply shivered and thought about how much she wished she was safe behind the castle walls right now. Through the trees they could make out two figures riding forward on horseback. They were both men, both about twenty years old, and both had shining swords hanging from their belts. Carelessly ignorant of the two girls hiding in the bushes, they tied their horses to two trees and walked forward to the stream.

Sophia fidgeted and her hand twitched. Helen slapped her across the face and leaned close to whisper in her ear, "Stop it! They'll hear us!"

One of the men looked up and began to scan his surroundings. He put his hand on the hilt of his sword and said something to his friend. The other man laughed and went back to munching on an apple he had procured from his bag. Still not convinced, the first man started walking around the clearing.

"Now see what you did?" Helen glanced at the sword on Sophia's hip. "Now would be a great time to use that thing."

Sophia's face paled. "Now? I...I can't use it now!"

"Why not?"

Sophia still hadn't told Helen about what happened when she stole the sword. "That just seems a little excessive, don't you think?"

Before Helen could say another word, they saw the man draw his sword and cautiously move toward their bush. With each step, he drew closer and closer; and Sophia's heart pounded louder and louder. Suddenly, Helen was bursting out from the bush with a loud war cry and a drawn sword. Sophia quickly followed, struggling to draw her mother's sword from the sheath.

To their surprise, the man chuckled and called out to his friend. "Philip, look what we have here! Two girls playing at being swordswomen!"

In fact, if they had been able to see themselves, they would have laughed too. Helen stood with her sword held in front of her. Her forehead was furrowed as though she was deep in thought. Sophia's sword was drawn but hanging loosely at her side. She was shaking and holding back tears. Both girls were dirty and shabby looking, with their clothes ruffled from the days of riding.

Helen, however, did not find the situation funny. "I'll do more than play if you do not tell me who you are right this instant!" She brandished her sword and took a fighting stance.

The man's sword met hers with a clash. He said nothing, simply smiled and dared her to fight with his eyes. Sophia jumped back out of the way as Helen swung her sword around, but it was once again blocked by the man's sword. No matter how Helen moved or faked or dodged, his sword was there to meet hers.

The other man, whose name was apparently Philip, sauntered over to Sophia. Surprised, she started to hold up her sword, but snagged the handle on her wrist and dropped it. Fumbling for her lost weapon, she bent over to grab it; but it was snatched up by Philip. Absolutely terrified, she stepped back and looked for something to throw at him.

It was at this moment that the first man knocked Helen's sword from her hand, catching her off balance, and causing her to fall backwards: right into Sophia! Both girls went tumbling backwards into the stream, followed by the sound of raucous laughter. Thankfully, the stream was shallow and slow-moving. Drenched to their toes, they both scrambled towards the bank, Helen berating Sophia the whole way. Philip stretched out his hand to help them out. Helen pushed it away. Sophia gratefully accepted it.

"I don't think we've been formally introduced. My name's Philip and this, overcautious and sword-happy man is my friend Duncan."

Wiping stray strands of wet hair from her eyes, Sophia smiled. "My name is Sophia and…"

"Mine is Helen, princess and heir apparent to the throne of Suffrom," Helen interrupted.

Both men smiled. Duncan handed her the sword he'd knocked from her hands and bowed regally. "Excuse me. We didn't realize we were in the presence of royalty," he laughed as he spoke. Helen snatched her sword from his outstretched hand and sheathed it, marching toward her horse and wringing her hair out as she went.

Philip stifled a laugh and returned Sophia's sword to her as well. "And are you her maidservant?"

Taken aback by his assumption, she angrily replied. "I'm her cousin, princess of Adven."

The two men exchanged a look before Duncan replied, "She wasn't joking?"

"Of course not! Why would anyone joke about a thing like that?" She sheathed her sword and put her hands on her hips. "And what would two vagabonds know about royalty anyway?"

They laughed. "Vagabonds? She called us vagabonds, Philip!"

"I told you that we looked the part! Should have listened when your mother told you to wash your clothes and shave your beard once in a while!"

"Well, at least I have a beard to shave!"

Sophia rolled her eyes at the exchange and started to wring out her dress. "At least it should be a little cleaner," she mumbled to herself.

Suddenly noticing that she was still there, Philip responded to her initial question. "We aren't vagabonds, milady. We're traveling swordsmen, adventurers you might say."

"And what do 'traveling swordsmen' do for a living besides swordfight with women travelers?"

"We travel from town to town and help people," Duncan explained. "Sometimes we just help with planting crops. Other times there's a criminal to be caught and stopped from hurting innocent people."

"Basically, it's an excuse to travel around Adven and see the world," Philip added.

"So, where are you headed now?"

"Actually, we were on our way to Suffrom. Wanted to explore new lands, meet new people, etc."

An idea popped into Sophia's head. Perhaps if she could convince these two to travel with them, Helen would be forced to travel at a more consistent pace. They would reach their destination faster, and the sooner they got to Suffrom...the sooner they could go back home! Besides the fact that Sophia would feel a lot better traveling in a group of four (with two men) than alone (with only two women); and obviously these two could handle their swords with skill.

"Sophia!" Helen's shrill beckoning voice broke through her thoughts and brought her back to the moment. Both men were staring at her puzzled.

"Would you excuse us for just one moment?" Sophia rushed over to their horses and grabbed Helen's hand before she could mount her horse. "Helen, just wait a minute. Listen to what I have to say before you go charging off again."

"Charging off again? If that's what you think you can just let me *charge off* and go wherever you please."

"Helen, please. They are going to Suffrom as well." She paused to let that sink in and then took a breath before speaking. "Perhaps we could ask them to travel with us?"

"Absolutely not! We don't need the assistance of two boys traveling as self-appointed heroes!"

"It would make me feel a lot better about this whole thing."

"What do we need them for? You and I have been trained to fight since we could stand. You have your mother's sword. What more do we need?"

Frustration overcame Sophia's attempt to remain calm. "What more do we need? Did you not witness what just took place? We could be lying dead in the river right now if they had actually meant us any harm. We are unprepared for what this world has to offer. God was looking out for us today, but..."

"Don't speak to me of God!" Both girls stared at each other in angry silence. Finally, Helen rolled her eyes and spoke, "Fine. If you want to drag two strange men along with us, that's fine with me; but I'm leaving in five minutes. If you're coming, you'll be ready then." She mounted her horse and rode towards the river to let him drink. Sophia walked back to where the two men had both mounted their own horses.

"Please excuse my cousin's rude behavior. She just doesn't trust strangers easily."

"And you, Princess, seem to trust them too easily. Lucky for you we mean no harm." Duncan's words urged caution, but his eyes danced with laughter and dangerous excitement.

38

"It's for this reason that I would entreat both of you to travel with us. We are also going to Suffrom, so my cousin may visit her homeland. It would be a great relief to myself if you would come with us, since you already said that was where you were going."

They exchanged meaningful glances while Sophia waited for an answer. It was Philip who replied, "It would be an honor, Princess, to ensure your safety until you reach your destination."

Joy flitted through Sophia's heart as she raced back to her horse. Things were finally beginning to turn around. Perhaps she would even make it home before the new year.

It was not until after the four riders were out of sight that a silent figure crept from the shadows of the trees. He was like a wraith, slipping in and out of the darkness in an attempt to disguise himself from wandering eyes. In fact, the only part Sophia would have seen had she glanced behind her was the glint of crooked teeth formed into a half smile.

Chapter Five

Crunch. Crunch. Crunch.

The sound of horse hooves on new grass, broken branches, and the occasional fallen leaf on the forest floor was calming and somehow peaceful. Wiping sweat from his brow in an attempt to wipe the worry from his heart, Edwin paused to look around him. He was in a somewhat familiar part of the forest; but it was far enough away from the castle that he couldn't have been here in many years. The girls' tracks were clear up until this point. He knew that Helen had tried to lose him in the river, but he was too good a tracker to be fooled by that.

Now he found himself confused by the story told by the horse prints in front of him. There were two horses with two small sets of footprints by them, obviously Helen and Sophia. They were beside two trees and then the girls' prints led down to the river. That part was clear. However, it was the second set of footprints in the clump of trees not that far away that filled him with concern. There were two horse prints and two sets of larger prints, obviously male. He could also see that there was a bit of a scuffle by the riverbank, which concerned him even more. Lastly, all four horses seemed to ride off into the distance as one group.

"What happened, girls?" Rubbing his beard in frustration, Edwin dismounted and inspected the ground once more. Suddenly, he saw an additional set of prints that had been disguised by the others. It came in from the forest and went back out the same way.

Crunch. Crunch. Crunch.

The sound of footsteps on new grass, broken branches, and the occasional fallen leaf on the forest floor alarmed him. He drew his sword and turned around to face his attacker; but before he could defend himself the hilt of a sword hit him in the back of the head. Surprised, he collapsed to the ground. The world began to go black, but Edwin could hear faint whispers and felt himself being thrown over the back of his horse.

Crunch. Crunch. Crunch.

The sound of horse hooves on new grass, broken branches, and the occasional fallen leaf on the forest floor lulled Edwin into a state of unconsciousness as his horse galloped far away from Helen and Sophia.

"So, what're you girls doing out in the middle of the forest in the first place?"

Sophia rolled her eyes. Maybe bringing these two along wasn't such a great idea after all. They'd done nothing but pepper her with questions since leaving the clearing. After a while, even Duncan grew tired of Philip's questions and rode beside Helen, who had yet to say anything, even to Sophia, since they'd started out again.

"I told you. We're traveling to Suffrom to visit Helen's homeland."

"But why aren't you traveling with an escort?"

"We can take care of ourselves."

He cracked a smile. "We've seen how well that works."

She wanted to punch him, but that wouldn't do her any good. "What about you? Why did you and Duncan decide to become 'traveling swordsman'?"

"I told you. We wanted to help people."

"Why?"

He shrugged. "I guess we thought it would please the gods."

"Oh." Somehow the idea that Philip and Duncan didn't believe in the One True God disappointed her. A deep sadness welled up inside for these two boys trying to do good, but not knowing why they wanted to in the first place. She was about to say something when Duncan stopped his horse and looked around. Helen's horse also pulled up short, and she turned around with her scowl still firmly in place.

"The sun is setting, we should probably settle in for the night."

Sophia nodded her assent and walked her horse to one of the trees surrounding the small clearing they found themselves in. Philip set to work starting a fire while Duncan took care of their two horses.

Helen led hers to a place a little way away from the others, and then sat down under the tree she'd selected. The four of them spoke very little as they shared their meager rations and prepared for bed. Helen went to sleep first, followed by Duncan. That left Sophia and Philip sitting by the dwindling fire, at last in silence.

"I'll take the first watch," Philip said as he threw down the stick he'd been toying with and watched the fire spark with the additional fuel. Sophia nodded and watched him as he strapped his sword to his side once again and started to walk away.

"Thank you."

She looked up with a puzzled expression on her face. "I haven't done anything."

"Thank you for putting up with my questions. I know that wasn't what you expected when you invited us along on this little adventure."

"It's fine, Philip. I just appreciate the company."

He glanced over to where Helen had segregated herself from the rest of the company. "She always this stubborn?"

"Yes," Sophia said emphatically.

"Her loss," he replied with a shrug.

"What loss?"

He smiled. "Her loss of the opportunity to spend time with someone as kind and thoughtful as you."

Before Sophia could answer, Philip was walking away from her very quickly. She could feel her cheeks burning red, and it wasn't from the heat of the fire.

The building was not impressive by any standard of architecture. In fact, it was probably simpler than some of the homes of the commonest peasants, at least from the outside. When you opened the wooden door to peer inside you saw dirt floors and simple furniture, but there were also decorations in bright purple cloth (the symbol of royalty) and brown (a symbol for common things). The two colors together created an interesting backdrop for those who entered, but it did not make the purpose clear. What did make the purpose apparent was the figure of an old man kneeling at the front of what could now be called a church. His hair was almost white, with only touches of gray, and he appeared shrunken and withered. But there was such a strength that seemed to emanate from him that it drew even the most skeptic person to him.

Solomon took in all of this in just a few short moments. He'd been in the little church many times. It was one of his favorite places to curl up and read a book or spend a few minutes to pray out loud, without the fear of someone else laughing at what he had to say. Today, he wasn't reading, and he wasn't concerned that others heard what he prayed. Today, he was praying for his sister, who they hadn't heard from in at least two weeks. And apparently Eli, his spiritual mentor, was joining him.

Hearing the door open and shut caused the old man to turn from his kneeling position and smile at the teenager young Solomon had become. He waved and beckoned him over to the front of the church. Gently, the boy sat down beside him.

"Are you praying for her too, Eli?"

"I have not stopped since I first heard."

"Me neither." Solomon shifted his weight from one knee to another and then back onto his heels. "I'm really worried about her, Eli…about both of them. Why would they do this? Don't they know how much it upsets everyone?"

"I'm sure Sophia didn't mean to upset anyone. That was why she left us a note, I believe."

"Even if Sophia didn't, Helen did," Solomon muttered under his breath.

If Eli heard the comment, he chose to ignore it. Instead, he bowed his head and resumed praying. But, even the peace of the chapel was not enough to calm Solomon's fears today. No matter what he tried to focus on, his thoughts seemed to wander. Prayers were the last things his brain wanted to think about. Eli sensed his discomfort and looked up at the distraught boy.

"Solomon, I remember a time almost 20 years ago when I could not seem to focus on my prayers, just like you. No matter what I did, every day I left my prayers feeling no better than before."

"What were you praying for? It couldn't have been Sophia, she wasn't born yet."

Eli laughed. "No, I wasn't praying for Sophia. I was praying for your mother."

"Mother? Why were you so concerned for her?"

"Much like Helen and Sophia, your mother had run away from the castle very suddenly. It was for a different reason, but the circumstances were similar. She was gone for almost a year before she returned, married and accompanied by a company of armed men. It was almost too much for me to bear. Every day she was gone, I prayed for her safe return. But I never felt that my prayers were heard. It left me very worried for her."

Solomon was hanging on every word of the story. "What did you do?"

"It wasn't until I prayed to the One True God that I began to feel less worried for her. Somehow, I knew He heard my prayers and would answer them. When your mother returned home, I thought at first that He too had failed me. She seemed lost to me because I did not approve of her marriage."

"You didn't like Father?"

A smile. "I didn't know him yet. I would grow to love him later, after I truly believed in the One True God." He shifted his weight and groaned from the pain that it caused. "You see, Solomon, the God that you and I believe in is the one who gives us hope for Sophia's safe return because He does listen to our prayers; and He does answer them. When you pray to Him, your worries will flee as His hope for answered prayer floods your spirit."

Solomon nodded thoughtfully. Just then, the door opened, and a serving maid entered the quiet room. She bowed her head respectfully and spoke to both men, "Her Majesty, Queen Katherine, sent me to inform you that lunch is ready. They are waiting for you in the Hall. Shall I tell them you'll be up shortly?"

Eli looked at Solomon for an answer. The look in his gentle eyes answered the unspoken question. "I believe we will be spending our lunch here, young lady. Tell Katherine that Solomon and I are interceding for Sophia today. We will join them for supper in a few hours."

The maid nodded and exited, pulling the door gently shut behind her.

"I think I'm ready to pray now, Eli."

"As am I, young man. As am I."

The next several days allowed the four travelers to get to know one another a little better, although it took a full two days before Helen would speak to anyone (and she never offered an apology when she did speak). Philip and Sophia especially found that they had quite a lot in common: sense of humor, outlook on life, and passion for helping people. The one thing that continued to bother Sophia was Philip's lack of belief in the same God that she believed in so strongly. Every time she tried to broach the subject, he changed the topic or gently teased her persistence.

"Why do you always laugh at me when I ask you that?"

"Laugh at what?" he asked mischievously.

"Whenever I ask what you think about the One True God! Surely you've heard of him?"

Philip pretended to think very hard, tilting his head this way and then that way. Finally, he said, "I think I've heard of Him once or twice perhaps."

Sophia rolled her eyes. Sometimes he was as bad as Solomon. "I know you've heard of Him. I can remember as a child all the traveling preachers that Father would send to spread the story of the One True God. Often they would return months later, ragged and worn, but excited and filled to overflowing with stories of the hearts and lives that God had changed."

"Duncan and I have come into contact with many people who claim to follow the One True God," his brow furrowed. "And not all of them have been good people."

Surprise registered across Sophia's face. "How could that be?" she asked incredulously.

Philip sighed. "I remember there was a small village that Duncan and I stumbled upon, no more than five or six families altogether. There was a man who claimed to be one of your Father's traveling preachers, I suppose. He talked a lot about God and how much He loves us, but mostly how we are to love others. He convinced the people of the village to give him as many of their possessions as they could, to give to those in need he said." Another sigh and a shake of the head. "I followed him on one of his 'giving trips' he called them, where he would distribute the gifts to the poor…But that wasn't really what he was doing. He was meeting another man in the forest, where he would sell everything he had collected from the village people and keep the money for himself." He looked at her with a very serious expression on his face. "I could never serve a God who condoned that. Duncan and I exposed what he was doing and ran him out of the village before moving on. The people were heartbroken over his deception, yet I suppose a few of them still claimed loyalty to your God, saying it wasn't what God would have wanted the man to do."

Sophia was about to explain further about the truth of God and the wrongness of what the man did, but Philip suddenly cracked a smile.

"I suppose I don't have to worry about ever getting conned like that with only what I can carry on my horse to my name…" he winked at her, "and a beautiful lady at my side."

She punched him playfully in the shoulder for that, and they laughed together.

"Looks like the two of them are enjoying themselves."

Helen looked over her shoulder to confirm Duncan's comment. Philip and Sophie were laughing about something, again. They always seemed to be laughing about something. What they found so funny, she was sure she would never know.

"I'm glad to see Philip enjoy himself with someone other than me," Duncan said with a smile. "Perhaps even something more?"

Helen rolled her eyes at the inferred question. "I think he'll find her less interested in something other than friendship than you might think. She's too innocent to think about things like that." She looked directly at Duncan. "Besides, haven't you both made it pretty clear that the two of you don't believe in the same God she does?"

"We don't." He shrugged. "Doesn't mean that won't change, but that's how it is for now. What about you?"

"What about me?"

"Well, you made it clear that it's the god 'she believes in'. You don't believe in him?"

"No, I don't."

Duncan waited for a little bit more of an explanation, but when nothing seemed forthcoming, he tried to lighten the mood. "Well then. I guess there's nothing keeping the two of us from getting to know one another, is there?"

She fixed him with a glare to emphasize her next words. "I think you'll find I'm even less interested than Sophia. Keep that in mind." Suddenly, she pulled up short and held out her hand for silence. "Did you hear that?"

"Hear what?" he asked, puzzled.

"I guess it was nothing. I just thought I heard some of the trees rustling over there…" She pointed to their left, but nothing seemed to jump out at them or stand out from the shadows of trees and trickles of light through the leaves.

"Maybe it was just the wind?" Duncan offered.

"Is everything alright?" Sophia called out from behind them.

"Everything's fine," Helen said crossly and clicked to her horse to start moving again.

Duncan followed a few paces behind her. Obviously, she didn't want to talk if she was that desperate to change the subject; so, he allowed them to ride in silence for the next several hours.

Chapter Six

The world was spinning around in little half circles as he opened his eyes. There were stars shining above him, but the moon was out of sight. A horses' whinny came from his left, accompanied by the gentle nudging of a horses' nose. With a groan he managed to pull himself to an upright position. Gently rubbing the back of his head, Edwin struggled to make sense of what had happened. He remembered riding after the girls, following them through the creek, tracking them to the clearing…where he'd found the girls' tracks with two more sets of tracks beside them! Now it was all coming back, just as he'd found another set of tracks coming in from the forest, someone had hit him on the back of the head! That was the last he could remember.

Blinking from the pain, he looked around him; but all he could see were trees, no landmark in sight. His horse was grazing on the grass next to him, seemingly happy for the respite. If only Edwin were as lucky. He could feel blood on the palm of his hand as he pulled it away from the back of his head. It was sticky, not running as though the wound was fresh. How long had he been unconscious? He remembered bits and pieces of his ride from…wherever he had found the girls' tracks to…wherever he was now; but it didn't give him enough to figure out how long he'd been riding or how far away he was from any semblance of civilization.

He looked at the stars again, hoping to see a familiar constellation that could point the way back to the castle. Any hope of finding the girls now had vanished when he'd been attacked. His only recourse now was to return to the castle and share what he had learned: that there was someone who desperately wanted Sophia and Helen to remain lost in the countryside of Adven.

Finally, he spotted a constellation he recognized: that of the knight holding his sword aloft. The star that illuminated the tip of the "blade" pointed the way due north. If Edwin followed that direction far enough, he should come upon a road that would lead him back to the castle.

Edwin poured some water out of the bag strapped to his saddle onto a piece of cloth he tore from the edge of his cloak. Tenderly, he pressed the cloth to the scrape on the back of his head and held it there. It stung, but the cooling effect of the water seemed to stop the blood flow…at least somewhat. He tore another piece off his cloak and tied the first piece in place. Eventually the cloth would no longer be cool, but then it would at least contain the blood until he could get somewhere where a doctor could look at it.

As he stood to his feet, the whole forest started spinning again, and he grabbed hold of his saddle to keep himself standing upright. The horse merely looked at him and then returned to grazing. Placing his left foot carefully in the stirrup, he swung himself over and pressed one hand to his head in an attempt to stop the throbbing the sudden movement caused. Pulling on the reins, he pointed his horse in the direction the sword blade indicated and spurred him into a canter. Later he would gallop, but for now a canter was as fast as his broken body could handle.

She was up earlier than the rest of the group. Her whole body ached, but inside she yearned to practice. After a quick bath in the nearby river, Sophia wandered a little way away from where the rest were sleeping. Slowly and carefully, she removed her mother's sword from its decorative scabbard. The soft swish that accompanied the motion was comforting and familiar. Today would have been her weekly lesson with Adam, and somehow it felt right to practice.

A parry here. A thrust there. Without a partner, it was a little more difficult than she anticipated; but she'd already made up her mind. Quickly running through the training exercises she normally did with Adam took only a few minutes. Soon she was pausing to catch her breath and trying to figure out what she would do next.

"Need a partner?"

Startled by the interruption, she dropped her sword; and it clattered against some rocks at her feet. "I'm sorry. I didn't hear you coming," she stuttered, blushing from ear to ear.

Philip laughed and reached for her sword. "I always seem to leave you speechless when it comes to that sword, don't I?" he laughed.

She punched him in the arm and took the sword from his other hand.

"My offer still stands," he said as he drew his own sword. "Need a partner?"

A moment or two passed before she raised her sword to the ready position. Philip hardly needed a second invitation, and his sword came flying at her unexpectedly. *Clash.* Her sword came up to meet his. She parried to her right. His sword stopped hers with a resounding *clang*.

"So, what's with the sword practice anyway?"

"Don't you want to be prepared? You know, in case we meet someone unexpected on our way?"

"All I can say is that you need the practice from what I saw a few days ago!"

A grunt accompanied her thrust, which he blocked just in time.

"Okay! Sore subject! I won't mention it again!"

"Good! Or you'll regret it!"

"You sounded a lot like your cousin when you said that."

Her anger got the better of her, and she swung haphazardly. Philip flicked her sword neatly out of her hand, and it landed in the grass a few feet away. Breathing hard and embarrassed that the same trick had gotten the best of her again, she fought to get air into her lungs. When her composure had returned, a frown formed on her face. "Did I really sound like Helen?"

"With the bitterness and the anger…yeah, just a bit."

"I'm sorry, Philip. I didn't mean it."

He reached for her sword. "I always seem to be picking this up for you." He started to hand it back to her, but then stopped when he saw the writing on the blade. After puzzling over it for a few minutes, he asked, "What does the writing mean?"

In her mind's eye, she could see the familiar script and embedded filigree. "It was very special to my Mother and Father. 'Place me like a seal over your heart, like a seal on your arm; for love is as strong as death, its jealousy unyielding as the grave. It burns like blazing fire, like a mighty flame.' It symbolized the love they had for each other...and for God."

"That's not what it says."

"What?"

"That's not what it says, Sophia."

"What do you mean, 'that's not what it says'?"

"Look. Look at the words! It's not what you said it was."

Puzzled, she took the sword from him and held the blade so that the light hit it without glaring and obscuring the words. She could hardly believe her eyes when it said,

Find rest, O my soul, in God alone; my hope comes from him.

He alone is my rock and my salvation; he is my fortress, I will not be shaken.

What did it mean? Suddenly, the incident in her parents' room came flooding back to her memory. The bright light and her burning hands. The guilt that crept into her heart when she was least expecting it. She had heard the story of the sword many times. How it was given to her mother by a mysterious, old woman in an obscure village on the outskirts of Adven. How it had protected her parents on several occasions before either she or Solomon were born. And yes, her mother had explained how it was imbued with God's power on that fateful day when she stole it while everyone was sleeping. But that still left the question...Why had the words changed, and what did they mean?

"Sophia?"

She started at the interruption to her thoughts. "Hmm?"

He stared at her with questioning eyes.

Instead of responding, she let the matter lie and walked away without saying another word.

With the curtains closed, the room felt musty; but that was how it had been for the past weeks. As dark as Katherine's mood, and just as closed off from the rest of the world. Michael had tried everything to get through to her, but all she would do is simply glance at the empty mantelpiece and sigh. On this particular afternoon, he found her once again sitting in her favorite chair by the window.

"Katherine?"

A half-hearted smile and a sideways glance were all he got in response.

"Katherine," he said with a sigh. "You can't keep yourself locked away like this." A pause. "Adam said you wouldn't let the servants bring you anything to eat this morning."

"I wasn't hungry," she whispered. The sound of her voice was hoarse and on the verge of breaking from crying.

Michael leaned against the back of the chair and gently put his hands on her shoulders. "Katherine…"

She shrugged off his hands and moved to the window, pulling one side of the curtains open as she did so. "Michael, don't worry about me. I'll be fine."

He shook his head. "I haven't seen you like this since…" He let the thought trail off.

"Since the war," Katherine finished. She didn't even glance back over her shoulder to see his reaction. This was where she really worried him.

"Katherine…"

"What?' Her response was tinged with anger. "I shouldn't be worried about her? She's my daughter, Michael!"

"Our daughter," he quietly corrected.

That brought a glance in his direction. But that was all. "There's just so much that could go wrong. She could get hurt or lost or…"

"Fall in love, get married, and come home with an army following after her?"

That brought a glare.

Michael came up behind her and carefully tied the curtains back, allowing the sunlight to brighten up the room. Then, he gently took her hands in his and turned her to face him.

"Katherine, I think you know how Eli must have felt when you ran off all those years ago."

"I didn't run off! I…"

He raised an eyebrow.

"Okay, so I ran off."

"And you turned out alright."

"Well, yes, but…"

"No buts, Katherine."

A roll of her eyes and a genuine smile. She glanced at the sun streaming through the window and the smile didn't leave. Her eyes followed along the wall until it came to the former resting place of her sword. Michael, seeing that the smile was about to disappear once more, turned her face towards him again.

"She'll be fine, Katherine."

Tears began to well up in her eyes as she started to protest, but Michael pulled her away from the window and towards the door.

"For now, let's just get something to eat. I'm famished!"

Katherine rolled her eyes and allowed herself to be led from the room.

"Oh, Michael! Have you seen Solomon today?"

"He's praying with Eli in the chapel."

She smiled. "I think I'll join them after lunch."

Dark shadows flitted through her mind as the nightmare overcame her peaceful sleep. Restlessly, she turned back and forth, rolling from one side to another. Images she didn't understand mixed with scenes from long forgotten stories, all of them frightening and horrific. And, a voice drifted in and out of her consciousness. It sounded close; but far away. Speaking in crackling whispers, she heard it say, "Fools. All of them fools to come here again. This is my domain!"

Helen awoke with a start and glanced around her. Philip, Duncan, and Sophia were all sleeping soundly around the now dwindling campfire. Scanning the immediate surroundings, she saw nothing but a shadow in the trees to her left. It seemed her nightmare had just been a very bad dream.

She would have returned to sleep were it not for the fact that the shadow she had dismissed as inconsequential moved. Alert as though it were midday instead of midnight, she carefully stole away from the clearing and towards the darkening forest around her. No longer could she see the shadow, but she could still sense whatever, or whomever, it belonged to was still close. Drawing her sword revealed barely a shimmer of reflected moonlight to light her way. Stealthily she crept along the edge of the camp, careful to not disturb the others. Following the line of trees around to the left, she found the spot where she had first noticed the shadow. There were a few broken branches on the forest floor; but very little else.

A scraping sound came from behind her, deeper into the forest. Helen turned around and raced toward it with sword extended. She felt something brush past her arm and she swept at it, thinking it was a fly or some sort of bat. Instead, a strong hand grasped her wrist and threw her to the ground. Winded and unable to call out for help, she lay helpless and waited for her assailant to make his next move. She could hear wheezy breathing from behind her head, obviously the first shadow she sensed. It seemed the wheezy voice was going to speak, but the man who had knocked her down was suddenly moving past her and dragging the other shadow with him. They were gone before she could regain her bearings.

Embarrassed and slightly ashamed of her foolish actions, she returned to the camp where the others were sleeping peacefully, completely unaware of the strange turn of events. Swallowing her pride, Helen started to wake Sophia; but it was Duncan who stirred.

"Helen? What's wrong?" he asked sleepily.

A steely smile crossed her face. "Nothing. Just checking on the fire. Go back to sleep."

He nodded and turned away from her. She in turn rolled her eyes and lay back down. "I'll just tell them tomorrow," she whispered as she slipped back into fitful dreams filled with shadows and raspy, wheezing voices.

"Let me see if I understand correctly," Philip said the next morning when they were lazily reclining around the long-dead fire. "You had a dream last night."

"It was not a dream!" Helen insisted.

"You had a dream," Philip continued, "and then you saw a shadow."

"And then the shadow knocked you down," Duncan finished.

"No! The other man with the shadow knocked me down. The shadow was probably an old man. I could hear his raspy, wheezy voice breathing down my neck when I was lying on the ground!"

Duncan looked at her skeptically. "In your dream there was a raspy voice."

Helen glanced at the ground. "Well, yes, but..."

"Are you sure it wasn't just a dream? You could have just been confused," Sophia added gently.

"I wasn't confused! I thought there was someone following us the other day!"

"Then why didn't you say anything?" Philip's skepticism revealed itself in his tone.

"Because I thought I was wrong! Duncan, you saw me last night!"

Duncan thought for a moment before adding his thoughts. "But you said you were just checking the fire."

She sighed and rolled her eyes. "I lied."

"How do we know you aren't lying now?"

"Philip! How dare you accuse Helen of making the whole thing up! Why would she?" Sophia protested.

The two boys exchanged skeptical looks but said nothing.

Helen fumed and let out a little squeal of frustration. "I can't believe that you think I'm lying!" She turned angrily to her cousin. "Sophia, I told you we shouldn't have brought them along! We were better alone. They're just getting in the way."

"Helen, you can't blame them. None of us saw anything."

"None of us *saw anything*? What's that supposed to mean, Sophia? You don't believe me either? Whose side are you on?"

"I'm not on anyone's side. I just…"

Philip interrupted the fight with a voice of reason. "Perhaps we could continue this conversation later?"

Helen's eyes flashed brightly, and she glared at him. "No, I don't want to finish this conversation later. I want to find out what Sophia really thinks. How she really feels about me."

Caught off guard and still angry, Sophia turned away from her cousin. "You're always overreacting. Making things a bigger deal than they really are. Can't we just drop it?"

Suddenly, she felt her arm being grabbed and \found herself being spun around to face the blazing anger of Helen. "Overreacting? *Overreacting?* Who was it that thought this was all a bad idea? Who lied to their parents to come with me? Who stole that sword sitting comfortably on your hip?"

Instinctively, her hand went to her mother's sword. The scalding, burning pain she experienced the night she stole it leapt into her mind with a renewed energy. Clenching her teeth to fight the rage and the incredible guilt threatening to overwhelm her better judgment, Sophia started to walk away; but Helen still gripped her arm. The rage and guilt won. "Helen, you really want to know what I think? I think you're selfish, conceited, and stuck up. I think you only care about yourself. I think that you've dragged me into a huge mess, led me into the middle of nowhere, and sabotaged any attempt I've made to talk you out of this madness!"

"So that's how you really feel? Well, you didn't have to come with me. You're just like everyone else   ! Always telling me what to do and telling me how I should act and not ever really caring about how I feel! In case you forgot, it's my father who's dead and buried."

"I can understand why your mother won't talk to you. You're completely unreasonable when you get like this."

It was at this moment that Philip and Duncan moved into action. The girls had been drawing dangerously close to ending this argument with drawn swords, so the boys grabbed them and pulled them apart.

"This is ridiculous! You girls ought to be ashamed of yourselves," Philip scolded. Sophia stopped struggling and he let her go; but Duncan continued to hold onto the enraged Helen. "You're family. Apologize and make up."

Neither girl responded.

"Okay, that didn't go as I envisioned."

Duncan offered a different suggestion. "Perhaps we could go back to the original argument? Did something happen to Helen last night?"

"Yes, it did," Helen seethed.

"Couldn't we retrace her steps and see if there's any evidence that her story is true?"

"Brilliant idea, Duncan. Let's go," Sophia said as she grabbed Philip's arm and dragged him into the forest. Duncan released Helen, who marched ahead without saying a word.

The group tromped into the forest with Helen in the lead, Sophia dragging Philip behind her, and Duncan following up the rear. In the sunlit afternoon, the forest seemed far less threatening than it had in the darkened night before. The quiet crunching of leaves coupled with birds singing would have made it a pleasant walk had moods been as bright as the surroundings.

"It was right about here," Helen said as she found a small patch of crumpled grass amidst the trees. "I pushed through that clump of branches; and he grabbed my arm right here."

The other three looked around for any sign of a struggle that would provide validity to Helen's story. Seeing nothing, Duncan shrugged. "I don't see anything, Helen. What happened next?"

Pantomiming the story as she told it, Helen continued, "He grabbed my arm and threw me to the ground right here." Her comments were punctuated by her dropping into the grass with a *thud*. She was about to continue when Duncan stopped her.

"Wait! Stay right where you are!"

Helen complied.

Duncan motioned for Sophia and Philip to stay put while he carefully circled the area Helen occupied. It was then that they saw it, nestled among the leaves: two sets of footprints on either side of Helen. Both sets appeared to belong to men because of their larger size. Both sets led away in the opposite direction they'd come from. There wasn't much else to see, but it was enough to prove Helen's story true.

When she realized that they finally believed her, Helen scrambled to her feet and dramatically nodded as a sort of "I told you so". Sophia rolled her eyes, and Philip glanced at his feet, slightly ashamed. Duncan started off in the direction the footprints led. Reluctantly, the rest of the group trailed after him. The trail ambled through the woods for several minutes and then opened into yet another unnoticed clearing. Here there were hoof prints from at least one horse, perhaps two.

"I say we follow them," Duncan said carefully. "We need to know why they've been following us."

When no one responded, Philip continued with the thought, "All in favor say aye?"

Again no one responded. Duncan shoved past the others with a mutter about getting the horses. Glancing quickly at Helen and seeing no protest on her face, Sophia felt obligated to speak.

"Wait!"

Duncan turned around and faced her rather stoically.

"Are you sure we even want to know who's following us? I mean, they're gone, right? We can just take a different route to Suffrom, can't we?"

"The quickest way to Suffrom follows those tracks," Duncan said.

"Besides," Philip added, "it's going to be dangerous until we know who's following us…"

"And why," Helen said darkly. "And why he attacked me."

There was something suspicious about the whole thing; but Sophia couldn't think of an alternative. "Alright, let's follow the tracks."

Another fifteen minutes, and the troupe set off again following a set of tracks with an unknown origin to an unknown destination.

Chapter Seven

So quiet. So still. All seemed at peace. The chapel could not understand the turmoil that raged inside of Solomon. Torn between two polar opposite concerns, his mind was unsettled. Confused by the entire situation, he tried to form his restless thoughts into prayers, but even the stillness of the chapel could not calm his trembling heart.

"I know it's selfish, God. I do. I want her to come back, but should I? I mean, if she doesn't come back..." He let his mind wander to what that would mean. If Sophia didn't return, he would be an only child. That certainly did have its advantages; but it also had its downfalls. Mainly one downfall: he would be the next in line to the throne. In all his sixteen years of life, he truly hadn't thought about it. With Sophia always around, the idea that he might someday rule Adven was an unneeded worry. Now, with the possibility that she might not return...

"But it's not possible! She will come back! Won't she, God?" His heart became an off-beat drum, hitting out a syncopated rhythm. Fear gripped him like a cold vise, and he didn't know what else to do but plead with God. "She has to come back, God! She just has to! What will we do without her? Mother and Father spend every waking moment worrying about her, Aunt Ralyn won't speak to anyone now, and Eli spends all his time in here." A pause. "And what about me, God? What am I supposed to do without her? Who am I gonna tease at breakfast for being late? Who will loan me new books to read?" A longer pause. "Who will run Adven after Mother and Father...?"

"Sophia will."

Nearly jumping out of his skin, Solomon turned around to see who answered his question. "Mother! I didn't know you were there."

Katherine floated through the empty room and sat down beside her son, arranging her skirts around her in a fan. It added a strange ambience to the whole disarray of his demeanor. Mother was always so peaceful in stressful situations, but he had seen the strain Sophia's disappearance had put on even her quiet calm. She placed her hand gently on Solomon's hand, which was quivering in his distress. "It's alright to be scared, Solomon."

He looked down at the ground.

She smiled the smile of a compassionate mother. "I know it's easier to worry, but it does help to talk about it."

The eyes that looked at her were that of a lost puppy instead of a sixteen-year-old boy. "It doesn't feel right."

"What doesn't feel right?"

"Thinking about myself when I should be thinking about Sophia."

"You really don't need to worry about her, Solomon. God will bring Sophia home to us."

"But what if He doesn't? Where does that leave me?"

Katherine said nothing but instead waited for him to continue.

After a long pause, Solomon continued tentatively, "Mother, I don't know how to run a kingdom. That was always going to be Sophia's part to play. I guess I never really knew what my part was, but it was never going to be King of Adven."

"Perhaps the question you should be asking is not what will you do if Sophia doesn't return, but what you will do if she does."

A puzzled look was her only response.

"What I mean is: what is your part to play? You said you never knew what it was, perhaps now is your opportunity to find out."

"Perhaps…"

Katherine's light laughter filled the tense air. "Don't look so serious, my son. All the problems of the world don't need to be solved in a day! Take a walk in the garden, read a book, do whatever you like," she ran her hand through his hair before standing to her feet. "Just stop worrying. God will take care of everything. In His own time."

Solomon stood and looked sheepishly at his mother, embarrassed for his sudden outburst of fear. Another moment passed before she opened her arms, and he fell into her embrace like a young child who has scraped his knee. Tears shimmered in Katherine's eyes as she spoke, "You will always be my little boy, Solomon; but every little boy must grow up. Perhaps this is your time to grow, but your father and I will be right here with you every step of the way." A single tear slipped over the edge of her eyes, "I promise."

It had been a week since they discovered the tracks and started following them. Already, Sophia was growing tired of it. Duncan and Helen hardly spoke, both completely focused on following the trail wherever it seemed to lead. At least there seemed to be some sort of silent camaraderie forming between the two of them. Philip on the other hand spoke entirely too much about everything and everyone. He seemed to be trying to make up for her sour mood. *Mother would be awfully disappointed to see me like this. I haven't laughed in days…*

"Sophia?"

Slightly annoyed at having her thoughts interrupted, she turned to face Philip, who rode comfortably beside her with half a silly grin plastered on his face. "What?"

"Wasn't that funny?"

She turned away and tried to discourage further conversation. "I wasn't listening."

He clicked to his horse to ride closer to hers and tried again. "Sophia, isn't there anything I can do to snap you out of this?"

"No."

He paused to regroup his thoughts. "Isn't this usually the point in time where you try and tell me something about the One True God," he joked.

Torn between wanting to glare at him and agree with him, Sophia chose to ignore him.

Their horses continued trotting on for a few moments before Philip tried again. "Please talk to me, Sophia. What's bothering you?"

"Nothing."

"You're lying."

"I am not!"

Philip gave her a look that said otherwise.

"Just drop it."

He sighed. "What happened to the Sophia I met a few weeks ago?"

Staring at Duncan and Helen riding stoically before her, she said softly, "She met reality. In reality, there's pain, suffering, and evil." Her voice grew so soft he could barely hear her add, "How can I find any joy in that?"

Before he could say anything else, they saw Duncan stop his horse and follow a few tracks into the forest. After a few moments, he returned with a frustrated look on his face. "The tracks are getting harder to read. It seems that the two of them, whoever they are, rode faster than the four of us could possibly keep up with, probably without stopping." A sigh of frustration followed this announcement.

"How far ahead of us are they?" Helen asked.

"These tracks are at least three days old. Originally, we were only perhaps half a day behind them."

"Well, then we can't stop tonight. We'll have to keep riding," Helen insisted.

"You've got to be joking."

Helen's glare affixed itself to Sophia. "And why would I be joking?"

"We've ridden for over twelve hours today. The horses are tired. *I'm* tired. We're stopping."

With that, Sophia jumped off her mount and wrapped the reins around a tree. "If you'll excuse me, I'm going to find a stream, so we can water the horses." Angrily, she stomped off, skirts twirling as if to punctuate her emphasis.

Helen mumbled angrily under her breath, but she also got off her horse and tied it to a tree. Duncan and Philip watched her stalk off in a different direction from where Sophia headed, still mumbling under her breath.

"A bit testy, aren't they?" Philip quipped.

Duncan glared at him in response.

"Hey! What did I do to make everyone so angry?"

"Just being you, Philip. Just being you."

Dropping the carefree demeanor entirely, Philip grabbed his friend's arm to keep him from walking away. "What's got into you, Duncan? I can understand why the girls are mad at me, but that doesn't have anything to do with you and me!"

Sighing and softening slightly, Duncan replied carefully, "I'm sorry, old friend. It's just…something about Helen. I just want her to be happy, you know? I don't want to see her so worried…"

A broad grin spread across Philip's face. "Duncan! Feeling some slight affection for this girl?" He snickered at the prospect.

"Don't even suggest it, Philip, or I will be mad at you."

Not taking the point, Philip started another jibe before Duncan stopped him with a thought.

"What about you and Sophia?"

The truth struck home then, and silence reigned while Philip tried to form coherent thoughts.

"Forget I said anything, my friend," he finally said, "Let's just go on being bachelors and leave these women to their quarrels."

It was at this opportune moment that both Helen and Sophia returned. Sophia carried a flask of water in one hand, while Helen carried an armload of firewood. Practically colliding with each other, they offered stern glares at both each other and the boys before stomping back into the woods.

"Deal," Duncan said, shaking his friend's hand before any more interruptions could ensue.

There was something sad about plucking the dead blooms off the various flowers in the garden instead of picking the flowers themselves. It was just one more reminder that fall was coming soon and winter coming close behind. Katherine's reflective mood was only slightly refreshing from her pensive mood of the last month. Even Michael had become worn out by her sadness and worry. Despite her comforting words to Solomon in the chapel, for the two weeks following that conversation she had worried all the more for her darling Sophia and misunderstood Helen.

Usually her garden walks raised her spirits and reminded her to have hope. However, the overall feeling of decay was making her feel even more depressed than ever. If only something would change for the better...

"Mother!"

"Queen Katherine!"

She turned around to see Solomon and Adam running towards her with excited looks on their faces. Solomon paused to catch his breath while Adam explained.

"Edwin has returned. He is waiting in the dining hall."

"And the girls?"

Adam shook his head. Solomon, having finally regained his breath, continued.

"He said he found their trail though! And he said there was something else, but he would only tell you and Father."

Dropping the dead blossoms from her hand, she picked up her skirts to keep from tripping and ran past them both. "Then let's go see what he's found! Solomon, go tell Eli the good news."

That is what I would call a change for the better.

The Edwin she saw before her was not what she expected when she finally arrived in the dining hall. Bedraggled and unshaven, the poor red head looked as though his horse had dragged him through a mud hole. Michael sat with him at the table wearing a furrowed brow. Whatever news Edwin brought was not good news by the looks of it. The two men glanced up from their conversation when she entered, and Edwin pushed aside an untouched plate of food.

"Katherine, did Adam tell you…?"

"He told me you had returned and that you had news to share," she pulled back a chair and sat down, putting her hand over Michael's to feel the warmth. "By the look on your face, it doesn't appear to be good news."

"I don't know what it is exactly, Your Majesty."

Nervous and expecting the worst, she gingerly sat beside her husband. His hand covered hers in an expression of comfort.

"Go ahead and explain, Edwin."

Running a hand through his hair and sighing, Edwin started his story. "I was following the girls' trail for several weeks, and everything appeared normal. Then I came to a clearing where there seemed to be two additional pairs of horse prints, and a struggle by the river."

Michael felt Katherine grip his hand tightly.

"Those four prints led off towards the southern border of Suffrom. I figured that's where Helen would head, and it appears she's the ringleader. Then it started to get strange. I found an additional set of prints that came from the forest and followed the rest of the group, but the prints were newer, fresher. Before I could investigate further, someone came up behind me and knocked me out."

Katherine let out a little gasp, and Michael returned the tightened grip.

"He must have thrown me over my horse and let her wander away because when I woke up, I didn't know where I was. I had to use the stars to find my way back here."

"Do you think you could find the place again?"

Sadly, Edwin shook his head. "I was simply following Helen and Sophia's tracks, which were certainly not in a straight line. I always knew I could find my way back to the castle, so I never worried about where I was."

"How then did you know they were heading towards the southern border of Suffrom?" Katherine questioned.

Michael answered before Edwin could. "I've ridden those roads many times over the past few years. The southern border of Suffrom is directly opposing the castle. If you ride south in any form or fashion, you will cross it. However, there are many ways to get there. Helen doesn't know the way, only a vague sensation of the direction she must take. The easiest border to find is that southern border. It's more an assumption than an observation."

"So, what do we do now?" Katherine's question went unanswered for several moments. Finally, Edwin started to speak, but Michael stopped him.

"I'm not sure there's anything we can do, other than what we have been doing: praying."

"What do you mean there's nothing we can do? We know where they're going!" Katherine objected.

"We always knew where they were going," Michael countered.

"Well, now we know for sure. We can send men to the southern border of Suffrom and catch them..."

"That border is miles long. It would take all of our men..."

"Then send them all! Send messengers to Suffrom for more men..."

"For two girls? There would be a revolt."

Edwin interrupted the argument with another thought. "What about those additional sets of prints?"

Michael looked thoughtful for a few minutes and rubbed his beard. Katherine knew better than to interject when he looked like this. This look accompanied by that action meant her husband was searching for an answer beyond himself. He was praying to the God they both served for guidance and direction.

Another moment of silence passed before Michael finally raised his head and answered the question. "I think there's still nothing we can do..."

"Nothing we can do? Michael, that's our *daughter*. We have to do something!"

"I think there's nothing we can do," he repeated, "because we don't know what the additional prints meant."

"Edwin, isn't there anything that you can tell us about the clearing where you were knocked out?"

"It was near a river or a stream of some sort…other than that, there weren't a whole lot of markings. I'm sorry, Your Majesty."

Katherine thought hard. In the back of her mind the description sounded familiar, vague though it was. She could feel Michael waiting for her support; but in her heart she couldn't abandon two of the people she loved most in the world. Searching for any reason to argue with his logic, she wracked her brain for the connecting thought that sounded so familiar. When it couldn't be found, she sighed and slowly nodded her head.

"You're right, Michael. There's nothing we can do at the moment."

Bang!

"Mother, you can't give up!"

Solomon's sudden entrance aroused them all and made Katherine jump from her seat in surprise. He rushed forward and grabbed her hands in an almost comically earnest fashion. Eli hustled in the door behind him and closed it once again.

"Please, Mother! Sophia needs you! You can't just leave her out there all alone!"

"Solomon…"

"Edwin can show you the way, can't he?"

A smile threatened to swallow her face, but she traded it for a more appropriate solemn expression. "If you were listening enough to hear that we weren't going to do anything, then you know that Edwin can't do that."

Bright red embarrassment covered his cheeks, but he pressed on. "Father, you didn't give up when Mother was kidnapped by that madman, did you? You rescued her!"

The fond memory brought a smile from Michael. "Yes, but that was different, Solomon."

"How? Because Mother had only been gone a few hours instead of a few weeks? Surely, there's a way!"

Before Michael could rebut the argument, Solomon was speaking again. "Edwin, you didn't give up when you were forced into the service of a stranger, did you?"

"No, I guess I didn't," Edwin mused.

"We have to have hope!" Solomon begged. He looked from each pair of eyes to the next in an attempt to plead his case. When there were no further responses, Eli walked up behind the boy and put a reassuring hand on his shoulder. The contrast of the fiery young man and the wizened old man was enough to put a smile on everyone's face.

"Of course, we have hope," Katherine said, "and no one said we're going to give up. We just don't have enough information to proceed at the moment." She bit her lip. In attempting to not agree with Michael, she had come to the same conclusion: they could do nothing but wait. Were it not for that continuing thought that tickled at the back of her mind, she would have felt completely at ease.

Like a far distant memory, she felt a nightmare returning. It darkened her eyes until the entire room faded away. Solomon, Eli, Michael, and Edwin became nothing but distracting voices in her ears. She could see a forest, specifically a clearing in the middle of a larger forest. The wind was howling and there was rain pouring down. Her hair whipped around her face and nearly blinded her. Still, she struggled forward in an attempt to get…wherever it was she was going. Suddenly, she tripped and fell onto a raised mound of dirt: a grave. Horrified, she pulled away, wiping her muddied hands on her dress. But this grave was familiar. A long-hidden memory was struggling to surface although her subconscious fought to keep it submerged. She stared at the grave, forcing herself to remember. A vision of her father floating through her memory, and it all made sense.

Then, she was falling…deep into the blackness, and a madman's laugh accompanied her descent. She covered her ears and screamed for it to stop; but the laughter just kept on coming. Mixed up memories danced in her mind, confusing her and making her dizzy. A face, not of her father, but of the madman who indirectly killed him filled her vision. Another scream erupted from her innermost being as she tried to run away from his piercing eyes.

"God, where are you?"

Her prayer of times long past forced the face away from her immediately, and she felt herself breathing hard. Soon, she became aware of Michael's voice drawing her back from the dark abyss.

"Katherine? Katherine? Answer me! Come back to me. Please, come back."

Shaking uncontrollably and feeling tears springing to her eyes, Katherine opened her eyes to find herself lying on the floor. Michael was holding her hand, while Solomon knelt on the other side of her with a concerned look on his face. Eli and Edwin stood a short distance away, also wearing concerned expressions. She shook her head and tried to sit up; but the world started spinning again so she lay back down.

"What happened, Mother?"

"I'm…I'm not really sure. It was like a dream," she shook her head. "There was a face…" Suddenly realization broke through her foggy vision. "Michael, wasn't there a clearing where we first met?"

"Yes," he said, confused.

"With a river close by?"

"Yes, what's all this about, Katherine?"

"Michael," she replied, with horror in her voice, "I think I know who's following Sophia."

Chapter Eight

The days moved very slowly, but the nights moved even slower. At least during the day they were riding non-stop after an unknown adversary. When it came time to stop for the night, there was nothing but silence and animosity between the four young people who gathered around the fire each night to share what little stores they had left. And when it was time to sleep for a few precious hours? Sophia was left alone with her thoughts for the entirety of the night, tossing and turning as fear mixed with regret swallowed up her consciousness.

She could remember as a child having nightmares that seemed so real the monsters they contained could have been right there in the room with her. They were nothing compared to the nightmares she was having now. Her mother used to say that dreams were important to remember once you woke up. They were one way that the One True God spoke to His people. However, Sophia tried every morning to block out the memory of the nightmares, afraid of what they might mean and knowing that they would only return again that night.

This night was no different. There was darkness all around her, so thick she could feel it like fog. Throwing her hands out in front of her, she tried to feel her way forward. It was like being locked in the deepest dungeon of the castle without even a candle to light the way.

Then suddenly a pinprick of light would appear, far away but in front of her. Greedily, Sophia would run to it so that she might reach it before the darkness extinguished it too. But even though she knew she had to be getting closer to it, the light never grew brighter or larger or clearer. It remained only a pinprick, until she was on top of it.

The thought occurred to her that it might not be real. Perhaps it was only a figment meant to mock her in this dream world. Her hand slowly reached out, but she drew it back almost immediately as the light scorched her palm. The pinprick now grew and was revealed to be her mother's sword…her sword. The words she thought she knew so well were emblazoned on the cold metal and glowed bright red against the yellow glow of the rest of the sword. But they were not the words her mother often quoted, they were the words Philip had read to her:

Find rest, O my soul, in God alone; my hope comes from him.

He alone is my rock and my salvation; he is my fortress, I will not be shaken.

The words echoed through the darkness and pushed it back from her, so it no longer crushed her spirit. In fact, the light spread all around her so that no darkness was left, and she lifted her arms to rejoice. But she felt dead inside even with the light swallowing her.

As soon as she recognized the deadness within her the light was extinguished and the darkness came back with a vengeance. Terrified, she screamed and called out for God.

"Where are you, God? Help me!"

Her voice sounded pathetic and did nothing to retract the darkness that enveloped her. Cries of sorrow wracked her body, and she shivered from the utter despair that overtook her.

It was then that she woke up, sweating and shivering, with tears running down her face. Wiping them away before anyone noticed she was awake, Sophia got up and walked away from her sleeping companions. She didn't want to know what the dreams meant, but she knew she couldn't afford to avoid this forever. Her left hand rested on the hilt of the sword attached to her belt. It was this sword that concerned her. Neither of her parents truly understood what this sword was capable of. It had saved their lives on multiple occasions, but it had done nothing for her. Only made her rush to the brink of insanity, where she now teetered.

Sophia found herself still pondering the mystery of the sword as the sun rose in the distance. Each day they rode closer and closer to the border between Suffrom and Adven. Each day she grew more and more frightened of the road they traveled on, further and further into the unknown.

The others woke up and stiffly stretched their aching limbs. Helen immediately moved to saddle her horse and prepared to leave while Duncan and Philip spoke to each other quietly. No one seemed to notice her, making her feel even more lonely. Shoving aside these rising emotions, Sophia picked herself up from the ground and prepared to leave with the others.

The foursome rode quietly for several hours, with Duncan and Philip occasionally stopping to check the trail for more tracks. Not a word passed between Helen and Sophia until Sophia quietly whispered, "I'm sorry about what I said. I was just angry."

Silence met her.

"I mean it, Helen. Being angry wasn't an excuse. I shouldn't have said what I did about your father...or Aunt Ralyn."

Moments ticked by. Then, "Apology accepted, Sophia. I'm sorry for goading you on." Then, Helen clicked her tongue to her horse, forcing it to ride alongside Duncan.

Philip took the opportunity to drop back from the two, pulling his horse up to speed with Sophia's. She offered a smile as a sort of a peace treaty. He responded in kind. Another span of silence filled the gap between them. Philip was the first to break it.

"I wanted to give the two of them some space."

A questioning glance from Sophia.

"Helen and Duncan. He may seem rough on the outside, but I think he's got a soft spot for your cousin." A quick glance forward, followed by a whisper, "Just don't tell him I said that."

She laughed and glanced forward also. Helen and Duncan were riding silently, side by side; but she could tell that he was looking at more than the tracks on the ground with questions running through his mind.

"They deserve each other."

There was another lull in conversation while Philip studied her, gauging her reaction. "So, how's reality treating you?"

A puzzled glance.

"You said there was no joy in reality last time we spoke. Changed your mind yet?"

She shook her head.

Philip waited, hoped for more, and then plunged ahead. "Duncan's not the only one with a soft spot."

A startled glance from Sophia.

"Perhaps I could change your mind about joy in reality?"

Sophia's horse came to a stop, and she did not respond.

"Sophia?" Philip's horse stopped also. His eyes followed hers as they stared off into the not so far away distance. Above the dark green treetops of the forest, the silky gray smoke of a burning fire drifted across the sky.

It did not take long for the four wearied travelers to find their way through the last few trees until they reached the smoke that Sophia saw. When they finally broke through the clearing, it was an unexpected sight that met their eyes. They found themselves on the outskirts of a tiny village. There was a large fire in the center of the houses with several women running to and fro cooking food for what appeared to be a large feast. Children ran in between the chaos playing tag. Teenage girls only a few years younger than Helen and Sophia clustered around the edges whispering to each other. The men were all working on putting up the frame of a house, and the sounds of their hammers filled the whole clearing.

One of the young women, who appeared to be about four years older than Sophia, turned away from watching the men and saw them. Her blue eyes and tussled blond curls brightened instantly as she saw them. She was sitting apart from the rest of the women, probably due to her rounded stomach that looked ready to pop any day. Supporting herself with one hand on her back, she strolled over to the group who stood still shocked at what they had stumbled on.

"Welcome to our village! You look as though you've traveled a long way. Come sit by the fire and rest," she winked. "There will be plenty of food tonight."

The four automatically followed her to where she motioned and collapsed. Some of the children led their horses away to what they assumed were stables. Someone brought them water, and the four drank greedily. The men finished their work as the sun began to set spreading bright crimsons and oranges with a splash of purple across the sky.

Then the dancing started. Celebratory dancing performed by everyone in the village, from child to elder. It was an organized chaos that relaxed everyone, even Helen, until each of them started to drift off to sleep. Everyone except Sophia, that is. She remained awake long after everyone else, trying to decide if all of it was a dream.

When Sophia awoke, she found herself lying on the ground next to the burnt-out fire ring. The others were still sleeping soundly alongside her in various states of repose. Helen lay on her stomach, face buried into her elbow. Duncan was on his back next to her, snoring loudly, which caused Sophia to snicker under her breath. She still hadn't quite gotten used to that. Philip was closest to her, curled up in a tiny ball; but his face was turned towards her. He was quite handsome when she looked at him now, resting peacefully without a care. His blonde hair fell in waves around his face with little curls that reminded her of a small child. She shook her head and sat up to look around. They were the only ones still sleeping; she could see the rest of the village had returned to their daily activities. All that remained of the night's activities were the fire pit and four sleeping travelers, rather three sleeping travelers and one very curious Sophia.

Just then she saw the young woman from the night before walking to the well in the center of the town. One hand held a bucket, while the other was gently rubbing her stomach. The bucket was obviously filled with water, but the woman was having trouble lifting it. Sophia jumped up from the ground and rushed over to help.

"Here, let me get that," she said picking up the bucket and offering a smile. The woman smiled in return.

"Thank you," she said, moving her hand from rubbing her stomach to rubbing her back. "I'm ready for this baby to get here any day now."

Sophia nodded, unsure of what to say next. The woman laughed. "I suppose you don't remember me, do you? That was a lot time ago!"

"What was a long time ago?"

"My name's Lilly."

Sophia simply looked at her puzzled and shifted the bucket from one hand to the other.

More laughter that sounded like the tinkling of wind chimes. "Why don't you bring the water to my house, and I'll explain there?"

She nodded. The two of them walked to a cottage on the other side of the town square, where a cluster of children were playing in front. A toddler boy rushed over to Lilly and threw his arms around her knees. She gently patted him on the head and then sent him off to play with the other children, who had all paused their game respectfully to wait for the boy's return. The whole town seemed to be a type of utopia, where everyone worked together. It was all rather confusing to Sophia, where even her home had been filled with inter-family strife because of Ralyn's attitude and Helen's antics.

Lilly motioned for Sophia to place the bucket on the table, which she did. The house was modest, at least what she could see of it. There was a table with four chairs around it, a small fireplace off to one side, and a rocking chair in the corner. A window gave a view to the children playing in the front yard. All in all, a very humble abode.

"I know you must be terribly confused about what's going on, where you are, and all that."

"I think I'd just settle for knowing who you are and how you think you know me."

A cheeky smile flashed across her host's face. "You're Princess Sophia, daughter of King Michael and Queen Katherine. The other woman in your party is Princess Helen, daughter of King Evan

76

and Queen Ralyn. I'm afraid I don't know who the young gentlemen are." Her eyes asked a question where there wasn't one.

Sophia chose to ignore the unspoken. "King Evan is dead."

"Yes, I'm aware of that. He died eighteen years ago, on the day you were born, leaving Queen Ralyn a permanent guest in your home and his daughter as heir apparent."

A puzzled look still wrinkled Sophia's brow. "How do you know all this?"

"I was there!"

A disbelieving glance.

"Do you remember a little girl who used to play nursemaid to you and Helen when you were quite young?"

"I had many servants and nursemaids growing up."

"Ah, but this would have been a very young girl, although she was older than you. Bright eyes, shining blonde hair, and unending enthusiasm?"

Nothing but a shrug to answer.

"Perhaps it was a very long time ago; and you were quite young." The young woman looked a touch crestfallen at such a disappointing end to her game. She ladled water into two mugs and handed one to Sophia, slowing sipping on the one in her own hand.

As Sophia drank, she wracked her memory for any glimpse of such a girl somewhere in her mind. Vaguely, a shadowing picture filled her mind. "There was one girl…"

The woman's eyes lit up excitedly, and the cheeky smile resumed its position plastered on her face. "Yes?"

"She taught me and Helen to climb the pear tree in the garden. We would take scrolls and books up to read while we sat in the branches and ate the pears!"

"Yes! And do you remember her name?"

A pause as Sophia dragged the long-lost name from her childhood memories. "Lilly? Yes, it was Lilly!" Another delighted pause before she squealed, "You're Lilly!"

The two women hugged, and Lilly let tears trickle down her cheek at the happy reunion. "Yes, it was I who taught you and Helen to climb the pear tree, although your mother wasn't happy about all the pears you ate that spoiled your supper!"

Sophia laughed at the recollection. But suddenly, her face clouded, and she looked at Lilly with concern. "But you left almost ten years ago. I never understood why you were suddenly gone."

The young woman shook her head and took a seat to rest her aching back. "I didn't *suddenly leave*. I said good-bye! You were just too young to completely understand what had happened; you were only eleven years old at the time."

"What happened?"

"One of your father's traveling preachers had stumbled on his old village. Do you remember the story?"

"How father ran away from Suffrom and finally surrendered to the One True God after making friends with a small village in Adven? Yes, he and Mother tell the story quite often. It was there that they first met."

"Well, in a clearing not far from here; but that's beside the point…"

"Wait. This is the village? The one Father always talks about?" Sophia glanced around her as if to voice her disappointment with her eyes. Somehow, she had expected something far different from such a legendary place.

"Yes," a smile, "and you're right. It does appear to be like any other village…from the outside."

Sophia blushed as Lilly continued her story.

"Anyway, one of your father's preachers had found this village in his wanderings and brought back a visitor to bring good wishes from the villagers to your family. You see, they did love him and your mother very much."

Sophia nodded in agreement. She vaguely remembered her mother and father being excited over news from old friends; but she had never truly understood, or honestly cared, what the fuss was about.

"The visitor was a young man named Peter, who was just about my age at the time. He stayed at the castle for several weeks, updating your parents on everything that had happened while they'd been away. It was during that time that we…"

"Fell in love?" Sophia finished with a smile.

A girlish giggle provided her answer. "When the time came for Peter to return to the village, I went with him as his wife! Eli married us with your parents' blessing."

"But what about your parents? And Peter's? Didn't they want to have a say in who he married?"

"My parents were thrilled with the match; and Peter's parents had passed away in an accident two years before we met. The only person he had left was a grandmother, who we knew would be extremely happy for us. Did your mother ever tell you about Maria?"

"Yes, of course. The woman who gave her the sword." Sophia's hand grabbed the hilt suddenly to assure her the sword was still safely strapped to her belt. Somehow being here in the village where it originated gave her hope that she could undo whatever mistake she'd made by stealing it. Perhaps Maria could help her! "Is she around here somewhere? I'd love to meet her."

A shadow crossed Lilly's bright face. "She died a few years back. I'm sorry, Sophia; but she was already quite old when your mother and father married. Peter and I were devastated and sent word to your parents, but I suppose it never reached them."

"Was she Peter's grandmother?" Sophia asked hesitantly.

Lilly nodded.

An uneasiness settled itself in Sophia's stomach. The one person who knew the most about this sword was dead. Now who could help her understand what was wrong with it? Assuming anything was wrong with it. Perhaps she didn't really know if anything was wrong, since she'd only used it a few times…and not in any particularly dire circumstances. But Lilly was talking again, so she snapped her mind back to the present conversation.

"I'm sorry, could you say that again?"

Lilly smiled. "Perhaps you were up too late enjoying the festivities last night. I noticed that you remained awake long after your friends did."

Sophia blushed. Then she tactfully changed the subject. "What was going on last night? Why the celebration?"

"One of our young couples gave birth to their first child. A boy."

"And that is worthy of celebration?"

"Every life is worthy of celebration," Lilly explained. "The One True God is the one who gives life, and therefore we celebrate it at every opportunity."

A nod accompanied by a smile before Sophia changed the subject again.

"I should go wake Helen and the others. She'll probably want to get started as soon as possible."

"Leaving so soon?" A frown brushed Lilly's face and darkened the brightness of her overall personality. "Why such a rush?"

"It's hard to explain…"

"Then perhaps you could do so over breakfast," she said as she walked to the fireplace and worked at starting a blaze. "Wake your friends and bring them back here. You can tell me your story while you eat."

"No, we couldn't possibly…"

But Lilly shoved her out the door and pushed her back toward the square before she could say one more word of argument.

Chapter Nine

The soft creak echoed down the stone hallways of the castle. Edwin grimaced and glanced around him to see if anyone had noticed, but the hall remained as empty as before. Hesitantly, he pulled the door the rest of the way open and stepped inside.

"Katherine was right," he whispered to himself as he looked around the room. Helen's clothes were strewn left and right with a chaotic disorder that mirrored his conflicting emotions. With every footstep, he could feel his heart pounding in time with his forward progress. *Thump. Thump. Thump.*

The balcony door was open with a slight breeze drifting inside. Edwin could feel the cool air brushing and calming his flushing face. And there she was, sitting with her back towards him, as always. She appeared to be as lifeless as a statue standing in the garden her unblinking eyes gazed out upon. Ralyn, Queen of Suffrom, mother of Helen…and something else Edwin couldn't bring himself to admit.

"Ralyn?" he softly whispered, praying for a response. There wasn't one.

He eased himself down to a kneeling position beside her chair, keeping his eyes on her face the whole time. "Ralyn? It's me, Edwin." She ignored him.

Forcing himself to focus on the task that had brought him here, Edwin pushed forward without the encouragement. "Ralyn, I…I just wanted to say…" A sigh. "This isn't easy, Ralyn."

He matched her gaze into the garden for the next few minutes. The flowers looked beautiful as they swayed gently with the breeze. Normally the garden would be filled with laughter and children running around under the watchful eyes of Katherine and Michael, whose favorite place was in fact the garden. However, with Sophia and Helen missing, the most frequented place seemed to currently be the chapel where Eli held court. Shaking his head, Edwin turned his attention once again to his silent companion.

"Do you remember when we used to sit on this balcony and watch Helen and Sophia play in the garden? They'd run all along the paths and jump in and out of the flowers and bushes doing who knows what. They were so young…so happy…I can hardly believe how fast they grew up."

He paused to see if any of his little rabbit trail was getting through. Nothing appeared to have changed. Ralyn still sat staring straight forward.

Edwin sighed. "I don't know how to say this, Ralyn, but…I'm sorry." He looked at her again, but there was still no change. The statue remained stiff. So, he continued.

"I'm sorry that they had to grow up. I'm sorry that life couldn't remain happy forever. I'm sorry that they ran away." He moved to kneel in front of her and placed his hands over hers, which were laid demurely on her lap. There was a slight shudder, but she didn't pull away. "I'm sorry I let you down, Ralyn. I tried to find them, but I failed. I should have looked harder, shouldn't have come back here until they were riding back with me. And if Katherine is right…" His voice trailed off as his eyes filled with tears. He stared at Ralyn's hands covered by his own, soft and white beneath his calloused tan. Edwin couldn't bring himself to look into her eyes.

"I wanted so much to be the one who found them, saved them, brought them back here…brought Helen back here…to you. I wanted you to, to look at me, to…to see me…" His words trailed off and the tears started to flow down his cheeks. For a few precious seconds his eyes remained on the two pairs of hands entwined in Ralyn's lap. Then, slowly but surely, his eyes bravely fought their way to meet her gaze. But instead of finding the distant gaze he anticipated, her soft chocolate brown irises were gazing at him instead of the garden. And what was more surprising was that for every tear that flowed down his face, another tear trickled down her cheek.

"Ralyn?"

"Edwin?" Her voice was hushed and crackly from lack of use. But it was still her voice; the one he knew so well.

"Please, please forgive me, Ralyn. There was nothing I could do..."

"Edwin, I was never angry with you. I could never be angry with you," she said as she placed her white hand on the tanned skin of his cheek, wiping away the tears as she did so.

"Then what happened? Ralyn, I...I love you. I thought you knew that."

Her tears were no longer trickling, but instead rushing down her face. "Edwin, it had nothing to do with you."

"Katherine? Michael?"

"No, it wasn't their fault either, as much as I hate to admit it."

"Then what was it?"

"It was me. I...I couldn't pretend anymore. I couldn't pretend that everything was alright, that I was alright, that I didn't hate what happened."

"Everyone hated what happened. It was tragic. It was unfair, but there was nothing anyone could have done."

"There was something He could have done."

"Who? Your husband?"

"No," she said softly, almost under her breath. "God could have saved him. He knew that I needed my husband to help me raise Helen, and He took him anyway. And now He's taken her too."

Edwin reached up and pressed his hand against her cheek, brushing loose strands of hair away from her face and wiping the tears from her eyes. "Don't you suppose that although Evan was gone...God gave you someone to replace him?"

"No one can replace Evan."

"Of course not. That's not what I meant. I simply meant that...I was there, Ralyn. I was there to help with Helen. Whenever you were tired, I took care of her. Whenever you needed someone to talk to, I was there to listen. Ralyn, I've always been here, just waiting for you to notice."

She didn't say anything for a few moments. But, eventually, she closed her eyes and pulled away from his touch. With a hint of regret chasing her every word, Ralyn whispered, "I'm sorry, Edwin."

"It's not too late. I still love you, Ralyn."

"I said, I'm sorry."

Their eyes met, and Edwin knew the truth within those cloudy brown irises. He stood and brushed away the dust and dirt that clung to his knees.

"I suppose it was too much to ask for forgiveness and love all in the same stretch of time."

"I told you, I was never angry with you. I'll always forgive you. I just can't forgive Him."

"And until you do, you won't allow the tiniest bit of happiness into your life?"

"What happiness is there in my life?"

Edwin shook his head and tried to keep the hurt out of his voice as he replied, "There could have been."

Without waiting for a response from her, he marched through the open balcony door and out into the hallway, slamming the door behind him. What he did not see was the statue crumbling into a tragic figure of a hardened woman, no longer happy with her solitude. Not that she ever really was. Ralyn slid from her chair and crouched in a crumpled position on the balcony floor. The breeze blew the hair from her face to reveal tear-streaked cheeks, and she did nothing to dry them.

"So, the woman who welcomed us last night is actually the girl who used to play with us when we were kids? Sophia, don't you think that seems a little far-fetched?"

Helen's skepticism was not particularly welcome once everyone had woken up. The boys were especially eager to eat the breakfast Lilly was preparing as they argued by the remnants of last night's fire. Only Helen was holding up any possibility of forward progress.

"I don't think anything seems far-fetched at the moment. Especially if there's food involved. Can't we argue about this later?"

Philip's stomach growled to punctuate his statement. Helen glared at him.

"Perhaps we could talk about this later. We'll all feel better after we eat something," Duncan suggested, with his eyes on Helen as he spoke.

Philip took her silence as assent and hopped up, urging Sophia to lead them to Lilly's house. Duncan continued to look at Helen, until he was satisfied that she would hold her tongue until later. He stood to his feet and offered her his hand to help her up. Surprisingly, she took it without hesitation.

"Your friend should learn to think with his head instead of his stomach," she whispered. "One of these days it just might get him into trouble."

"Philip doesn't often think with his head. More often he thinks with his heart," Duncan replied. He paused. "It's surprising how often his heart has been right over these past few years."

"I've never had much success with that line of thought."

A rare smile flickered across Duncan's face. He realized Helen was still holding his hand. "Perhaps you should try."

He led the way as the couple trailed behind Sophia and Philip, walking hand in hand.

Breakfast had never tasted so good as it did in Lilly's humble kitchen that morning. Lilly's young son, Thomas, had greeted the visitors quickly and taken his food outside to give them privacy. The other children had dispersed to eat breakfast at their own homes, agreeing to meet again to finish the game before lunch. Lilly had peppered the two girls with questions, most of which were answered by Sophia. The two boys listened with interest for a while and then changed the subject when the opportunity presented itself.

"Lilly, we're actually on our way to Suffrom. Is there anyone who knows the best way to get there?" Duncan's sudden reminder of why they were at the village in the first place flooded the room like a darkening shadow that even Lilly's bright eyes could not lighten.

"Of course, there are several of our men that have travelled to the edges of Suffrom to trade with the other villages there. I'm sure one of them would be happy to accompany you there on their next journey."

"I'm afraid we won't be staying much longer," Helen said with an edge to her voice.

"Oh?" Lilly looked around at the four faces, only one of whom seemed to look her in the eye. "Why might that be?"

Sophia started to speak, but then closed her mouth and looked at the ground. Philip and Duncan exchanged quick glances before Duncan said, "We believe we're being followed."

"Followed?"

"Someone attacked me the other night. Or rather, two someones. We're all eager to get away from them as soon as possible."

"Wouldn't staying here throw them off your trail? Would whoever is following you be expecting you to stop?"

"Actually," Philip said hesitantly, "we tracked them here. That was how we stumbled on your village last night."

"I see," Lilly said, pondering the words as much as the young man who said them. "And so, you believe that the men who attacked you and have apparently been following you live here?"

It was the first time the words had been spoken, but as soon as they were shared…the four weary travelers looked at each other in shock. It hadn't occurred to them that the place they assumed was a safe haven was actually the home of Helen's attacker. Well, no one had thought about it, except perhaps Helen. And now the thought terrified them.

Sophia was the first to recover from the shock. "That can't be right, can it? Mother and Father always spoke so highly of this place! I can't imagine that someone from here would…"

"But that's what you just implied, Philip was it?" A smirk crossed Lilly's face. "What else could you mean by saying the tracks led here?"

"I…I didn't mean…well, I didn't think I meant…"

Suddenly, Lilly's face changed from smiling to a grimace. A tiny squeak of pain let out through her clenched teeth.

"Lilly?" Sophia's voice edged on panic as she leapt from her seat and rushed to her childhood friend. "What's wrong?"

"Nothing," she breathed heavily. "Nothing is wrong." She continued to breath heavily for a few minutes and couldn't speak.

Duncan and Philip gently pushed Sophia out of the way and helped Lilly into a chair. She had been standing throughout the conversation, leaving the chairs to her guests; but when she suddenly seemed gripped by pain, her body had crumpled to the floor. Helen remained seated and seemed unmoved by the commotion.

Lilly opened her mouth to speak again, but instead of words came a scream that rebounded off everyone's ear drums and left a ringing in their ears. Thomas heard from outside the door and came running in.

"Mama?" The boy shoved Duncan and Philip out of his way as he rushed to his mother's side. "Mama? Mama?" he repeated.

"Thomas," Lilly managed through her clenched jaw, "go get Papa from the field. Tell him it's time."

Before she could say anything else or give any further instructions, he was running out the door and letting it bang shut behind him. Sophia finally regained her senses and said, "Time for what?"

Tears were streaming from Lilly's eyes, squeezed shut in an attempt to mask the pain. "Time for another celebration," she said before arching her back and screaming once more.

Sophia paced nervously outside the small house after the visitors had been banished with the arrival of Lilly's husband and the midwife. Thomas had run off to tell his friends that a new brother or sister was about to be born, leaving the four young people at a loss for what to do. Helen had continued to remain unmoved by the sudden chaos all around her and sat demurely on the ground with Duncan beside her. Both were watching Philip's failed attempts at calming Sophia's frazzled nerves.

"Sophia, you're acting like this is the first time a child has ever been born. It's not even Lilly's first child. She's going to be fine."

"Of course, I know all that. It just doesn't make it any less nerve wracking."

"She was just as nervous when Solomon was born," Helen said in a curt tone of voice. Philip glanced as her, frustrated and curious at the same time.

"Who's Solomon?"

"My brother. And, I was only 2 years old when he was born; of course, I was nervous!" Sophia's answer shot barbs at Helen's hard face.

"I wouldn't know," she shot back with a piercing glance the boys couldn't interpret. Helen and Sophia stayed like that, locked in a glaring contest of wills. It was Philip who once again broke it up.

"Sophia, why don't you just sit down for a few minutes? You won't help anything by wearing a hole in the ground."

She sighed and collapsed next to Philip on the ground. "I know. But, it's not just the baby that's got me worried…it's what Lilly said, about the people who attacked Helen being from here. I mean, it just doesn't feel right for this placed to be…" She trailed off as she searched for a word. When one wasn't forthcoming, she let the sentence die.

A sudden cry from inside the house made everyone jump. Lilly's screams ricocheted out of the house and into the surrounding street. The boys grimaced and glanced at each other, Sophia shot a concerned look at the closed door, and Helen stared at the ground. There was silence in between the short cries, which were eventually broken by the squealing cries of a newborn baby. With a look of relief, Sophia hopped up from the ground, pulling Philip with her, and headed towards the door.

"I wouldn't go in just yet, young lady."

Sophia turned around with a look of surprise to address the speaker.

A middle-aged man with an attractive face stood looking at the huddled group of young adults. His eyes were kind, but slightly weary, as though he had been through hardships more than once in his life. He was well-built and stood with his muscular arms crossed over his chest.

"If Lilly is anything like my wife, she won't want a crowd of people surrounding her just yet."

Sophia hung her head with a slight feeling of shame that she hadn't thought of that first. "Of course. I was only concerned…"

"Lilly is strong, as will her child be."

There was a lull in the conversation as no one knew what to say next. It was Phillip who once again broke the silence with an extended hand towards the stranger. "I don't believe we've met. My name's Phillip."

"Mine is Jacob," he replied with his own hand extended. "You four are the visitors that rode into town last night, if I'm not mistaken?"

Sophia nodded. Helen gave her a quick warning look. "Why is it any of your concern?" she said tersely.

He laughed. "I meant no harm. I was more than happy to have four additional guests to celebrate the birth of my son."

"It was your son that was being celebrated last night? Congratulations!" Sophia said quickly before Helen could stop her.

"Thank you," Jacob said with a smile. "I will pass on your congratulations to my wife as well."

"What's his name?" Sophia asked excitedly. She felt Phillip put a hand on her elbow, but she shook it away. Helen grunted another warning behind her head.

"Seth. His name is Seth."

Another startled cry of a newborn babe filled the town square. Thomas appeared around the corner and pushed past the group to peer in the front window, pushing back the closed curtain as he did so. He grinned so wide it went from ear to ear as he turned to face the crowd behind him, "Mother is motioning for us to come in!" He didn't wait for anyone to follow his instructions, and instead pushed open the door with youthful exuberance.

Duncan held the door open for Helen to walk inside with a final sideways glance at Jacob. Phillip placed his hand once again on Sophia's elbow as his friend walked inside the house. "It was nice meeting you, Jacob. Perhaps we'll see you again before we leave?"

"Perhaps you will. It was nice meeting you as well, Phillip & Sophia. Pass along congratulations from myself and my wife to Lilly."

"We will," Sophia answered, but Jacob was already turning away from them to leave. She started to follow Duncan and Helen into the house, but Phillip stopped her with a tight grip on her arm. "Let me go, Phillip. You're hurting me!"

"You need to learn to be a little less trusting of strangers."

"What are you talking about? Lilly must know Jacob and his wife. They live right here in the village!"

"Perhaps. But still. *We* don't know anything about him or anything about this village as a matter of fact."

"It's where my parents met. Lilly grew up in my castle, was my friend! How can you act like we walked into a village of ruffians? They've not done anything that might make us think badly of them! In fact, they've been incredibly welcoming. I know now why my Mother and Father miss this place so much. It's not bad at all, as a matter of fact."

"Don't get too comfortable. We'll be leaving as soon as we can," Phillip said as he turned to open the door for her.

"What has gotten into you? Why are you so against this place all of a sudden?" Sophia realized he still hand one hand on her elbow, which she roughly shoved away.

Phillip leaned close to her ear and whispered so only she could hear his startling words. "He knew your name, Sophia; and I only told him mine."

Chapter Ten

Preparations for another celebration were in full swing by the time Phillip and Duncan managed to escape from the house filled now with well-wishers. Sophia had insisted she stay should Lilly need any help, but Phillip knew she was avoiding him. Clearly, Helen would have much preferred making her own preparations to leave; but after a quiet conference with Duncan, she begrudgingly agreed to stay with Sophia. That left the boys to their own devices, which at the moment meant simply getting as far away from the chaos as possible.

"So, what was Sophia's reaction when you told her your suspicions about Jacob?" Duncan asked quietly.

Phillip shook his head. "I didn't even get that far. I merely mentioned that he knew her name, and she refused to acknowledge it. She insisted I heard wrong and would have locked me outside if it wouldn't have made a scene."

"I thought she believed Helen's story?"

"I think she does. She just doesn't want to believe that the person who attacked her could come from this village. I don't understand."

"Haven't you ever wanted to believe in something, Phillip? This place seems to mean a lot to Sophia's family."

Phillip shook his head again and took a long look at his friend. "I haven't been anywhere or known anyone long enough to believe in them. My whole life has been filled with people who want you to believe in them, but then always end up disappointing you. Well, you know my parents…"

With a slow nod, Duncan silently put a hand on his friend's shoulder and stopped walking. "You believe Sophia, don't you?"

"I don't know. I want to, but she just…"

"Thinks with her heart? Sounds like someone I know."

A light punch accompanied Duncan's smile. Phillip looked sheepishly at the ground.

"You really care about her, don't you?"

Mumbling accompanied by a sheepish shrug was Duncan's only answer.

A long pause followed, during which the boys listened to the sounds of the village all around them. There were children playing and bothering their parents who were rapidly cooking and cleaning to prepare for the celebration tonight. Lilly; her husband, Peter; their son, Thomas; and, of course, the new little one would be the guests of honor. As such, they simply would get to enjoy all the hard work of the other members of the village. The celebration would be an especially large one, Thomas had explained, since Maria had been a well-respected member of the community. Tonight at the celebration, Lilly would also reveal the name of their new child, a daughter (something which had initially disappointed Thomas). Then, just as before, the celebration would last long into the night with singing, dancing, eating, and fellowship.

"We should leave in the morning. It will only do more harm to stay longer. I know Helen will agree," Duncan said softly.

Phillip nodded. "I'll tell Sophia a little later, after she's had some time with Lilly. Perhaps she'll be a little more willing to listen to reason."

"If not, perhaps you can appeal to her heart," Duncan suggested. There wasn't a trace of sarcasm or malice in his words. Only a brotherly understanding of his friend's torn emotions.

Once again, Phillip nodded, and the pair continued walking in silence through the hustle and bustle all around them.

"I am pleased to introduce to you our second child, and first daughter, Maria," Lilly smiled at Peter as she explained the name choice. "In honor of Peter's grandmother, Maria, a Godly woman and a great leader of our village in her time. May our daughter grow to be like her in every manner! Thank God for this new life!"

"Thank God for this new life!" repeated the crowd with a resounding cry. Then everyone applauded and cheered as Peter kissed Lilly on the cheek and then his new daughter gently on the forehead.

Sophia clapped perhaps louder than anyone while Phillip, Duncan, and Helen looked on. She still had not decided when to tell Phillip that she'd forgiven him. Actually, she'd never really been mad at him, only at her continuing doubts which he happened to voice. It had unnerved her when she realized that Jacob already knew her name; but there could be a hundred reasons for that! Lilly or Peter might have mentioned who she was after everyone had gone to bed last night. Or maybe Phillip was confused, and he had introduced her to Jacob at the beginning of the conversation.

She shook her head. It was all just a little too much. No one would notice if she just slipped away, not now that the villagers were starting to separate back out into their little groups anyway. Besides, she just didn't feel like facing Helen's told-you-so attitude or Duncan's stoic disapproving silence. And she certainly didn't feel like facing Phillip's question she'd pretended not to hear. *Couldn't I change your mind about joy in reality?* If reality included the inability to trust the people her mother and father believed so strongly in, she had no interest in that or any other related reality.

With a quick glance, she noticed that for the moment no one was paying attention to her. Phillip and Duncan were quietly removed off to the side, whispering back and forth; while Helen had found an out of the way place to sit down and ignore everyone. She turned from her place and started to walk back to Lilly's house. *Perhaps I can just sit at Lilly's kitchen table and sort out my thoughts for a while. Then I'll be able to face everyone again.*

A stone skittered across the ground as her boot came into contact with it. It bounced a few feet in front of her and then to the left. *I feel like that stone. First one way and then another. First to Suffrom, but now bounce here to the village where my parents met. Who knows where I'll bounce to next?*

"Oomph," Sophia said as she suddenly collided with another body coming in the opposite direction. "I'm so sorry!"

A soft chuckle. "Aren't you headed in the wrong direction, Sophia?"

She tried to stifle an unexpected wave of panic that flooded her senses. "Jacob! I'm...well...I'm just a little tired is all."

"It's too early to be tired. The celebration has just begun! I know that Lilly wouldn't want you to miss it."

Sophia felt warning bells going off in her head, mostly with Phillip's disapproving look accompanying them. She tried to end the conversation quickly. "I'm sure she'll understand. We've traveled a long way."

"Yes, you certainly have. Have you much farther to travel?"

Another alarm sounded in her mind. "I'm not sure to be honest."

"Don't you know where you're going?"

"Sort of," she said with what she hoped was a nonchalant shrug of her shoulders. There was something about all of Jacob's questions that were just making her more and more nervous. He didn't need to know their plans. And how did he know how far they'd traveled?

"Would you like me to walk with you to Lilly's home? I'm assuming that's where you were going?" Jacob's smile appeared friendly enough, but Sophia was still unsure.

"No, I wouldn't dream of pulling you away from the celebration. Your wife is looking for you, I'm sure."

"She is resting at home with Seth actually. I think she wore herself out yesterday with our own celebrating."

"Oh," said Sophia, quickly searching for another excuse to get away. "Well, anyway, it's not that far; and I'd hate to trouble you..."

"It's no trouble at all!" He offered his arm, which Sophia begrudgingly took.

They walked for a few minutes in grateful silence on Sophia's part. When they got close to Lilly's house, she tried to lose her uninvited escort one more time.

"I know where I'm going. Her house is just up this way...I'm sure I can make it on my own now..."

"You know," Jacob said seriously while still staring straight ahead, "with everyone at the celebration; it's really not safe for you to be walking around in the dark alone. Even with that fancy sword on your belt."

Her free hand instinctively went for the hilt of her mother's sword. Cool to the touch, it did nothing to relieve the swelling panic inside her. *How did he know about the sword? Or, did he know? He just called it "fancy"...that doesn't mean anything, right?*

With his free hand, Jacob pushed open Lilly's door. "Here you are, safe and sound! Are you sure you'll be alright here alone until the others get back?"

"Yes, quite sure," she said quickly, already urging the man back out the door.

"Would you like me to get Helen for you? To keep you company?"

Her cheeks flushed red and the panic continued to crescendo to a peak within her steadily beating heart. "No, that won't be necessary."

His smile faded quite suddenly. "Sophia, is something wrong? You look pale. Are you feeling alright?"

"Yes, of course. I'm fine. Just fine. Thank you for walking me home." She hurriedly closed the door and sat down with her back to it. Soon she heard the sounds of Jacob's feet walking away, kicking stones and newly fallen leaves around as he went. Tears of fear, kept inside thus far, started to trickle down her cheeks as she breathed out a sigh of relief.

Duncan is right. We've got to get out of here. Sooner rather than later. I can't stand these people anymore! The never-ending smiles and laughter grated on Helen's nerves as she watched the crowd of villagers ebb and flow around the happy couple. Peter and Lilly appeared radiant in the firelight, and all the attention certainly helped. Thomas hadn't left his mother's side the whole night, playing the role of protective older brother quite well even with only a few hours of practice. Sophia had been the same way with

Solomon, although she had been a little too young to understand why all her baby brother ever did was cry and sleep. She used to torture her parents with questions about when he could come out to play with her and Helen.

She yawned and stretched as she looked around once more. Duncan and Phillip had sauntered away earlier, saying they were going off to prepare the horses for the journey in the morning. When she'd asked if Sophia was coming with them, Phillip had said "yes" rather hurriedly and then avoided any further questions. Clearly, he hadn't informed her about the plan just yet.

"Helen?"

The unfamiliar voice startled her. "Yes, Jacob, was it?"

Standing with his hands in his pockets, he didn't appear as threatening as this afternoon. *Perhaps Phillip isn't paranoid. Perhaps he's just jealous. Although this guy is clearly taken already...*

"Where is your wife? Enjoying the celebration somewhere around here I suppose?" Helen asked sleepily.

"Resting at home actually," he replied, taking his hands out of his pockets to nervously wring them out in front of him. "Helen, I think Sophia might be in trouble."

Instantly, Helen was on her feet with her hand on her sword. "What do you mean? Where is she?" A quick glance around revealed no sign of her.

"She went back to Lilly's, and..."

"Why would she do that?"

"She said she was feeling tired..."

Helen groaned and looked around for Phillip and Duncan. When they were apparently nowhere in sight, she let out another sigh. "Jacob, will you tell Phillip and Duncan where I've gone?" She decided she simply had to trust him for the moment. After all, he had brought her word about Sophia, right?

With a silent nod, he turned and walked away; while she found herself walking in the opposite direction back into the village.

Her hands fumbled around in the dark for a candle. *Surely Lilly has one sitting around here somewhere.* Sophia wiped sweat from her brow that instantly felt like ice on her hand. It certainly was starting to feel like fall during these chillier nights. *We'll need to make sure we take plenty of blankets with us when we leave.* But her thoughts weren't on their departure, only of the here and now as her feelings of panic had not yet subsided.

A scratching sound outside the door stopped her in her tracks. "Hello?" she whispered tentatively. "Jacob? Helen? Phillip?" With each unanswered query, she grew more and more startled. Still she searched desperately for a candle.

Footsteps almost sounded like they were approaching the door…but it didn't open. Sophia stopped and stood still, listening to all the sounds of the night. Now, there were nothing but crickets and the sounds of the celebration in the distance.

She gave up her search and crept to the door, pressing her back against it once more. Her hand gripped the hilt of her sword, pleading with God for it to work should she need it. But to her utter dismay, her pleas were met with nothing it seemed; for the sword stayed as cold and dead as any other sword in her father's armory. *God, where are you? Please, I…*

Her prayer was interrupted by a sudden hand covering her mouth with a cloth of some kind. She struggled to break free from his grip, but it was surprisingly strong. Her left hand flew up to pull the cloth away from her face; causing her attacker to push even harder against her nose and mouth. A muffled scream was all she could do under the circumstances.

The room grew cloudy, and she felt her grip on the hand slipping. Sophia struggled to grasp her sword, but it only clattered to the ground when she tried to unsheathe it. Feeling a sudden release, the cloth pulled away, and her weight pulled her to the ground in a crumpled heap. Her hand stretched out to search for her sword or anything else to fend off her attacker; but the night was so dark, and she was so tired. She heard the door creak open and hit her in the back, causing her to lurch forward into an awkward kneeling position.

Sophia felt her eyes drooping, and the raspy breath of her attacker on the back of her neck.

Helen burst into Lilly's house to see nothing but a deserted kitchen with a few overturned chairs. Something that looked like a dish cloth was sitting on the floor. She sheathed her drawn sword and picked up the cloth. It felt damp, as though some sort of liquid had been spilled or mopped up by it. When she put it to her nose, she quickly pulled the horrid scent away from her nose and sniffed wildly to rid her senses of it.

"Sophia?" Helen called, not expecting an answer. "Sophia, are you in here? Jacob sent me to get you. Hey, answer me!"

Footsteps behind her caused her to draw her sword and unleash a fierce battle cry as she spun around to meet the unknown assailant.

"Whoa!" Phillip cried as he jumped back from Helen's attack. "What's going on here? Where's Sophia?"

Duncan pushed past Phillip into the small, now slightly disheveled house. "Helen, are you alright?"

"Yes, of course. It's Sophia we've got to worry about. She's gone!"

"What do you mean gone?" Phillip's voice cracked with unintentional emotion, and even though the situation was quite serious, Helen found herself trying not to laugh. He sounded like a boy going through puberty.

Catching her muffled attempt at laughter, Duncan smiled and then tactfully turned to the matter at hand. "Jacob told us you had come back for her, and that she might be in trouble. But she was already gone when you arrived?"

"Yes, the only thing I found was this," Helen said, gingerly holding out the dish cloth. "It smells awful."

Duncan sniffed and then passed it to Phillip, who sniffed and immediately started choking from the stink. "What is that?" he said in between coughs.

"I don't know, but this doesn't look good for Sophia," Duncan replied.

Just then Jacob arrived at the house, standing just outside the doorframe. With a quick glance around, he surmised the extent of the situation and stepped forward. "Did you find anything?"

"Nothing," Helen said tersely, "except that smelly cloth in Phillip's hand."

Jacob took one smell and pulled away. Phillip dropped the cloth back on the floor where they'd found it. He wiped his hand on his shirt in an attempt to rid it of the smell. "We've got to go after her."

"Go after her? We don't even know where she is, how she got there, or why!" Helen was already spiraling back into one of her darkest moods. As much as Sophia annoyed her, she was really the only family she had left...considering her mother was practically dead to her. "Jacob, did she say if anything was bothering her?" As much as she wanted to continue distrusting this man, he appeared to be the last link to her missing cousin.

He shook his head, and she groaned in frustration. She kicked the chair next to her, causing it to topple over. It was then that she noticed something. The floor of the house was packed down dirt, but it was still covered with indentations from the table, chairs, and other people who'd walked through the room. With the birth this afternoon there had been a steady stream of people in and out, leaving all kinds of footprints going in and out of the front door.

"Look," Helen said as she knelt on the floor. She pointed to a light set of footprints accompanied what appeared to be something dragged across the floor, something like a body. It led, not out the front door, but into the bedroom and over to the window. Lilly's home was close to one of the edges of the village, meaning the bedroom window had a beautiful view of the surrounding forest. "Whoever took her, took her into the forest through this window."

"Well, now we know where she went. We've got to go after her!" Phillip said, already headed back out the front door. "Duncan and I already prepared the horses. We were going to leave in the morning anyway." The last comment was directed at Jacob, who still stood somewhat blocking the doorway.

"I'm coming with you."

"You weren't invited," Phillip said gruffly as he attempted to push past the man; but Jacob was stronger.

"You'll need someone who knows the area."

"We'll be just fine," Phillip insisted through gritted teeth.

Duncan put his hand on his friend's shoulder and pulled him away from the door. "May I speak to you for a moment?" Phillip nodded, while still giving a steely glare in Jacob's direction.

Helen, Duncan, and Phillip retreated to the bedroom. Duncan spoke first. "I don't trust him either, Phillip, but if we want to find Sophia speed is a necessity."

"Which is why we are wasting time talking here. We should leave immediately!"

"I know, and we will. But we should take Jacob with us. He does know the area better than we do. We'll find her faster that way."

"Absolutely not! For all we know, *he* could have taken her and then fabricated a story about walking her home. I don't trust him at all."

Duncan stared at Phillip for a few minutes before turning to Helen. "What do you think? Do we take him or leave him?"

Helen pondered the dilemma for a few minutes. She looked from Phillip to Duncan and back to Phillip again. She heaved a heavy sigh before saying, "I think we have to bring him with us, as much as I hate to admit it." Her next words were directed to Phillip. "If you care about my cousin at all, then you have to know that the longer we delay here debating lessens the chance that you will ever see her again."

Phillip clenched his teeth and stomped out of the bedroom, rudely shoving past Jacob to head towards the now dwindling fire of the celebration.

There was a slight breeze that whipped through Phillip's hair and face as he made his way across the town square and over to the horses tied to a post just outside the village. His teeth were clenched, and his hands continued to remain gripped into fists. *How dare that man...Jacob...* He couldn't even finish the thought. Anger raged through every part of his body. *I know he had something to do with this. He probably kidnapped her himself!*

His thoughts were interrupted by a gentle touch on his shoulder, causing him to spin around so violently that he almost knocked the baby out of Lilly's arms. "Lilly! I'm...I'm sorry...I didn't see you there."

"Where's Sophia? I wanted to speak with her before you left."

"Before we left? How did you..."

Lilly smiled and shifted the baby in her arms. "I am not blind. I saw you and Duncan preparing the horses earlier. Did you think I'd let you slip away without so much as a good-bye?"

"I'm sorry," he said sheepishly. "It's nothing against you, really. There's just some other...things going on now."

"Things between you and Sophia?"

He blushed. "What makes you say that?"

Another smile, accompanied by a soft coo from Maria. "The look in your eyes is the same as when I look at Peter. Does she know how you feel?"

"I don't know...maybe...but, Lilly, there's something else you should know."

"Yes?"

He sighed. "Sophia's gone."

An arched eyebrow. "Gone?"

Phillip leaned forward and whispered, "Kidnapped. Someone has taken her. Helen, Duncan, and I are headed out to go find her."

"With Jacob?"

He jumped back, surprised. "Why would you say that?"

There was a short pause before Lilly answered, leaning forward to whisper as he'd done. "Be careful. Jacob is new to our village, having only been here a few years. He brought his wife with him, but they have not made many friends during their time here. Peter has always been suspicious of him. I noticed he had taken an interest in you and Sophia and the rest of your party, which has me worried. He acts as though he knows you already."

"He knew Sophia's name when I had not yet introduced her."

Maria started to fuss, pulling at her mother's dress and letting out little whimpering cries of distress. Lilly put her up on her shoulder and began gently rubbing her back. Eventually she drifted back to sleep. "Be careful, Phillip. That's all I can say. Would you like Peter to go with you?"

"No, Jacob might be suspicious of that."

Lilly nodded and motioned with her head towards the quickly approaching threesome of Helen, Duncan, and Jacob. "Good luck, my friend. Find her quickly."

Phillip nodded and turned his attention to the horses, hurrying to get everything ready before the rest of the group arrived.

Chapter Eleven

The mist of the previous evening faded into the early grayness of the morning sunrise. Sophia ached all over, as though she'd been dragged through a canyon filled with spikey rocks. *Perhaps I have been.* She looked around her, but her gaze was limited by the fact that there was a large rope wrapped several times around her chest and stomach, tying her to the tree behind her back. As if that weren't enough, her hands were bound tightly in front of her.

All she could tell was that she was in the middle of a forest. The streaks of orange and yellow sunlight that danced across the trees told her that she couldn't be all that far from the village. The terrain looked very similar, albeit much more forested. Beyond that, there were no more landmarks that could possibly give her a clue as to her location. She sighed in frustration.

"Awake now, are we?" came a raspy voice from behind her. Sophia stiffened and felt her breaths come in short quick gasps. She instinctively felt for her sword at her side, but of course he'd confiscated it.

"You didn't think I'd leave that little knife for you to cut yourself free, did you?" She could hear the hints of a smile from the owner of the raspy voice. As her panic level rose, so did the sounds of her own breathing…sounding raspier and raspier by the minute.

"Breathe deeply, dear. Can't have you passing out before the fun begins." Every hair on her body stood on end with the implied threat ringing in her ears. Unbidden, a single tear traced down her left cheek. She closed her eyes and wished with all her heart that this was a terrible dream, that she would wake up and hear Solomon in the hallway calling her down to breakfast. When she did open her eyes, all she heard was the sound of her panicking heartbeat and heavy breathing. Another tear slipped down her cheek.

Suddenly, she felt hands touching the side of her face from behind. What surprised her the most was their texture: the hands were the wrinkled hands of an old man, which must be the reason for the raspy voice. A scrap of rough cloth pressed over her face clouded her vision and interrupted her analysis.

"Can't take any chances with you, my dear. I've waited a long time for this."

Sophia felt the cloth tighten over her eyes and could feel those wrinkled hands tying knots behind her head. Her heartbeat increased, and her breathing again came in short, quick gasps. "What did I ever do to you?" she whispered, trying to control the tears that continued to trickle down her cheeks. "Why are you doing this to me?"

She felt the presence move from behind her to in front of her, moving in close to her face although she could not see his. The hot air of his breath made her sick to her stomach as he breathed deeply in and out. "You'll know soon enough."

With that, she found herself alone again. More alone than she had ever been in her life. Sophia could no longer control her tears and allowed them to flow freely, sobbing into the blindfold without restraint. *God...I don't even know what to say.* And that realization made her feel even more alone than before.

"Can't we go any faster?"

Jacob jerked his head back over his shoulder and gave Phillip a confused look. "Do you want to find your friend or not?"

Like I believe you're really taking me to her. Phillip glared at him and then looked down at the ground. They'd been riding for hours, but they seemed to be making very little progress. Every few minutes, Jacob would force them all to stop and check the ground for tracks. *Something Duncan or I could have easily done. What do we need him for?* The further they rode, the more the anger inside Phillip grew and grew. Now it was bubbling just beneath the surface ready to explode at any moment. *I can keep my emotions under control as long as Jacob doesn't do anything else to annoy me.*

"Besides, I think we should stop for now. The horses need a rest, and there's a stream nearby. Perhaps I'll be able to pick up the trail from there."

So much for controlling my emotions. "Excuse me?" Phillip snapped. He could feel his face turning a bright cherry red as the anger bubbled over. "You want to stop? Sophia is out there, getting further and further away; and you want to *stop*?"

"Phillip," there was a warning edged in Duncan's voice as he spoke. "Can I speak with you for a moment?"

A near growl was Phillip's reply as he dismounted. Jacob was already leading his horse towards the aforementioned stream. Duncan dismounted and handed his reigns to Helen, who stepped forward to take them. She'd already dismounted when the argument first started. Their hands touched for a few brief seconds, perhaps longer than necessary in Phillip's way of thinking. "Follow Jacob. Phillip and I will be along shortly." Helen briefly nodded and started to walk away. She paused and held out her free hand towards Phillip.

"Give me your reigns too...unless you'd rather have Jacob take care of your horse?" He saw a faint trace of a smile pulling at the corners of her mouth. If it was supposed to be a joke, it wasn't a very funny one. He practically threw the reigns at her and stormed away with Duncan on his heels.

"You can't continue to let your feelings for Sophia interfere with our attempts to find her," Duncan said softly.

"How dare you think I'm trying to interfere with anything! I want to find her more than anyone!"

"I didn't say you were trying to interfere; I made the statement that you *are* interfering. For example, I'm here arguing with you instead of helping to take care of the horses so that we can get moving again."

"You can't possibly trust Jacob," Phillip pointed out. "You're the most suspicious person I know."

"I don't trust him," Duncan replied. "But right now, he needs to feel that someone does." He cocked his head to one side and smirked. "And he's certainly not going to buy you suddenly putting your trust in him. Not with how vocally opposed to his presence you've been."

That stopped Phillip for a moment. He mulled it over in his mind before speaking again. "What are you up to, Duncan?"

"Nothing. Nothing at all," he said, smirk still firmly in place. "But we shouldn't leave Helen with Jacob alone for too long. Who knows what she might do if he gets on her nerves."

Now it was Phillip's turn to crack a smile. "She's seemed a bit more mellow the past couple of days. There something else you're up to, Duncan?"

"Nothing. Nothing at all," he replied. But, before he turned away, Phillip caught the smirk turn to a brief, but genuine, smile.

Sophia didn't know how long she sobbed, but apparently it was long enough that she fell asleep again. What woke her was a rough slap on her cheek by the same wrinkled hands that had accosted her in the night. She woke with a start, and the first thing she noticed was that her cheeks were now dry. *Must've slept longer than I thought.* The second thing she noticed was that her stomach was growling, and her throat felt like sandpaper.

"Hungry? Thirsty? If you're not, too bad!" The voice chuckled. The rough feeling of a canteen pressed against her lips. Before she could completely process what was happening, she felt liquid flowing over her lips and choking her as it went down. She coughed to try and clear her throat, but her kidnapper kept pouring the water. Sophia shook her head free of the canteen and finally coughed the phlegm free from her throat.

"Here," the raspy voice commanded. She felt a small loaf of bread pressed into her bound hands. "Eat."

"How am I supposed to eat while I'm tied to a tree?" She'd intended for her question to come out sarcastic and fierce, like Helen in one of her moods; but instead it came out trembling and weak. Sophia internally kicked herself. *First the crying and now this. What kind of a princess am I? Can't even stand up for myself in front of my kidnapper.* When she realized the absurdness of that line of thought, she shook her head.

She suddenly felt the ropes around her chest slip free. "Eat. Then I tie you back up," the voice explained. Without giving him a chance to change his mind, she shoved the bread as best she could into her mouth, careful not to drop it in her haste. It was dry and had a hard crust, but gradually the pains in her stomach began to decrease. When there was nothing left but crumbs, the wrinkled hands pressed the canteen into her empty palms. "Drink."

Sophia found herself trying to relish each sip of water as it poured down her throat, at a much slower pace this time. She knew that as soon as the canteen was empty, or her kidnapper decided she'd had enough to drink, that she would be tied to the tree again. *Think, how can I use this situation to my advantage? What would mother do in this situation? How can I escape?*

"Enough," the raspy voice said as it slapped the canteen out of her hand. She heard it slap on the ground and felt the spilled remainder of the water soaking the bottom of her dress. *So much for that thought.* She wanted to roll her eyes or make a witty comment that would put him in his place. But without her summons, at her eyes appeared those unwanted tears again.

She heard the raspy voice chuckle. "Crying again are we, dear? I think I'm going to have to gag you this time around; you were a little loud last time. Wouldn't want anyone trying to come and save you, now would we?"

His words were like a numbing agent to her entire body. Sophia felt her bound hands drop in front of her like they were made of stone. Every muscle in her relaxed, and she would have collapsed to the ground if he hadn't shoved her hard against the tree to retie the ropes around her. *He's surprisingly strong.* She felt a rough piece of cloth, similar to the blindfold she still wore, being shoved in her mouth and tied behind her head. *He's going to give me a headache with all these knots behind my head.* The thought was almost funny.

She heard his footsteps moving away from her without another word; and she felt her tears still streaming down her cheeks. A sob caught in her throat, choked by the gag in her mouth. *God, where are you? I'm so alone.*

He awoke with a start, sweat running down his face like tears, streaking in frantic little paths like rivers. His hands went to his cheek and felt the dampness there. *Maybe it was tears*. He let out a low moan and covered his face with his hands, resting a moment before throwing the blankets off.

"I fell asleep in my clothes. No wonder I'm sweating," Solomon said with a shake of his head. A glance out the window revealed that the moon was still shining. "It must be the middle of the night," he whispered to himself. "Why am I awake?"

Sophia.

Her name sent a shiver and an ache through every bone in his body. He'd spent day and night in the chapel for almost a week since Edwin had brought his uncertain news about his sister. Eli and Mother, even Father, had tried to get him to return to the castle for his meals and to rest. This was the first night he'd finally been convinced to return to his own bed to sleep. He was too exhausted to argue and finally fell asleep, still wearing his clothes apparently.

Sophia.

He shook his head, attempting to wake himself from whatever nightmare he was apparently having. He stretched his arms over his head. His back cracked, and he let out another moan.

Solomon. You must pray for Sophia.

"That's what I've been doing," Solomon said as he yawned. He didn't really know why he said it out loud. It just felt like the right thing to do.

She needs you. She is alone.

A slice of panic shot through him, finally jarring him completely awake. Outside he could hear the quiet sound of crickets chirping, but they were completely drowned out by the sound of his own heartbeat, pounding in his ears. He could feel his knees start to shake, and he placed his hands on them in an attempt to settle them. They continued to shake despite his efforts.

She is alone. She needs you.

"Sophia?" Even his voice was shaking, unsure of itself. He buried his face in his hands for a few moments, the fear washing over him anew. "Sophia, where are you?"

She is alone. She needs you. She needs me.

Solomon recognized this still, small voice inside him. It brought warmth to his heart that stifled the fear trying to rise up in its place. "God?"

When he didn't hear an answer, Solomon slipped from his bed to the floor, kneeling and burying his face in the blankets as he did so. "God, I don't know where Sophia is. But wherever she is, let her know that she's not alone. I love her. You love her. Everyone here loves her." The words couldn't come for a moment as he felt himself starting to break down. He took a few deep breaths before continuing. "Keep her safe, God. Bring her home. Please, whatever it takes…just bring her home."

There was nothing but the sound of crickets and his deep breathing for a few minutes. The moonlight still shone in through the window, illuminating the tousled sheets and disorderly room. Solomon finally stood to his feet, wiping a few stray tears from his eyes. He strode to the closet and started changing into some clean clothes. He sniffed the shirt in his hand before putting it on and wrinkled his nose. "Well, they're cleaner at least." He'd probably forgotten to ask the maids to do his laundry the past couple of weeks with everything going on.

Quickly, he grabbed a pair of boots from under the bed and slipped them on. His footsteps sounded hollow and echoed through the hallway as he made his way from his bedroom. His breathing had returned to normal, but he still felt driven to keep moving.

You're not alone, Sophia. Just hold on for a little while longer.

The crisp night air hit his face, brushing his hair back and away from his eyes. He breathed deeply and felt his body start to relax. As he made his way across the moonlit yard, he felt himself being watched. A soldier on night duty approached him. "Prince Solomon," he said with a bow. "May I be of assistance?"

Solomon shook his head. "I appreciate your concern, but I am simply headed to the church for the remainder of the evening. You may return to your position."

"I will stand watch for you, sire."

"That's really not necessary," Solomon insisted. He felt strange having soldiers concerned about his safety. Always had. Probably always would. "If you wish to do something useful, you may pray for the Princess Sophia."

The soldier bowed his head in respect. "Of course, sire. I will pray for her as I stand watch over the church."

Solomon smiled at the soldier's persistence. "I'll be just inside if anyone asks for me, please send them in right away."

The soldier nodded and took his place outside the church doors, bowing his head slightly in prayer. Solomon could feel a sense of pride welling up inside him. He pushed open the doors, just as the moon began to set and the first tentacles of sunlight started to poke its way through the clouds.

You are not alone.

Sophia jerked from sleep abruptly, trying to process the whisper in her mind. She'd spent most of the night silently crying but had finally drifted off to sleep sometime in the middle of the night from what she could guess. It was hard to tell with the blindfold still in place. Now, she could vaguely feel the warmth of the sun on the part of her face not covered by the blindfold or the gag, as well as on her hands. In fact, her hands were beginning to feel sunburned; she could feel the skin starting to itch and peel. She tried to twist her hands to gain some flexibility back, but that caused her to let out a muffled cry of pain through the gag.

"Awake again, are we? Good, it's time to go for a little walk." The raspy voice had a hint of a cruel smile as it spoke.

Sophia felt the ropes around her feet come loose first. She hadn't realized how swollen her ankles must be from being constricted for so long. Carefully, she stretched and rolled them as her kidnapper cut apart the ropes strapping her to the tree.

Before she could move at all, she felt a knife at her throat and the trickle of fresh blood flowing down from where the knife pressed against her skin.

"Just to be clear, my dear. I will kill you if you try to escape. I think that much is obvious. I will also kill you if you attempt to free your hands or remove the blindfold or the gag. If that information is clear, nod once."

Sophia nodded once, her chin touching the skin of the wrinkled hand that grasped the knife currently at her throat. The pressure released, and she felt herself let out a sigh, choking on the gag as she did so. She left her hands resting in front of her, resisting the urge to pull the blindfold away from her face. It was really starting to itch.

Suddenly, she felt herself falling. *Well, of course, I've been standing up against this tree for…* A sudden panic filled her. *How long have I been here? One day? Two days? It can't have been more than two days, right?* The panic lodged itself in her throat, and it took everything within her to keep breathing normally as her body slumped to the ground. She allowed herself to lean against the tree for support.

"Don't get used to it," the raspy voice said with annoyance. She felt him reaching down and pulling at her bound hands, wrapping an additional rope around her wrist and knotting it tightly. She whimpered against her will.

"Too tight, dear?" the voice asked with a sarcastic tone attached. "Can't have my dog getting off her leash, now can I?"

So that's what this is? A leash?

She felt her hands being tugged forward by the newly attached "leash". Her feet and legs begged her to resist the tug, but there was no strength within her to fight it. She felt her arms lift first and then her shoulders. Begrudgingly, the rest of her body followed suit.

"Come, we'll spend most of today walking; it's best to get a head start."

111

And with that, Sophia felt herself be pulled along like a dog at the end of her kidnapper's leash. *God, where are you? I'm so alone.*

You're not alone, she heard a still small voice whisper. But perhaps it was just her imagination.

Chapter Twelve

"You've been awfully quiet today," Duncan whispered.

"Not much to say," Helen replied. "Either that or Phillip's said it all already."

"Was that a joke? Did you actually just make a joke?"

A smile twisted Helen's face as she tried to stifle it. "No, a statement of fact. Does that friend of yours ever stop talking?"

"Not usually," Duncan's face contorted into a frown. "Which is why it worries me that he's been so quiet the last few hours."

Helen nodded. The three of them, along with Jacob, had been riding most of the day. Jacob had insisted that he'd found some sort of trail, which Phillip seemed to completely disbelieve; but Duncan had argued that it seemed at least possible. That was when Phillip had lapsed into complete silence. Of course, he could tell that his friend still trusted him; but he wasn't sure how much of his silence was playing along and truly simmering with rage. He'd never seen him this emotional about something, or someone, before.

"He really cares about her, doesn't he?" Helen whispered.

Duncan broke from his reverie to turn to her. The breeze was gently blowing stray strands from her braid out of her face, and her eyes looked not at him but down at her horse. She really was beautiful, this gentle and caring side of her that he was just beginning to see. "It would appear that way."

She nodded. "She deserves to have someone care about her that way."

"And you?"

Her eyes left the horse to meet his. "Me what?"

Duncan tried to look as serious as possible as he quietly asked, "Do you deserve to have someone care about you that way?"

She didn't say anything for a long moment. Her eyes were merely locked with his, searching, darting back and forth, wanting to find the hidden question…and maybe the answer as well.

"No."

"No?"

She broke her gaze and stared back down at her horse. "No, I don't deserve to have someone care about me that way."

He started to say something else, but Helen interrupted his train of thought.

"My mother blamed everyone for my father's death, even me for some time. Although I know it had nothing to do with me, I still felt somehow responsible. But then I grew up." She paused, struggling to find the words to explain her emotions. Her tone was even and straight, no hint of weakness or tension aside from the clipped and precise nature of her words. "I realized the real culprit of who was to blame for my father's death and my mother's depression." She glanced at Duncan to gauge his reaction thus far. "That God that Sophia and Lilly and all of those villagers talk about. He was responsible for what happened. He could have stopped it, and He didn't. That makes Him directly responsible."

"No."

"No?" His reaction surprised her. He'd shown no interest in any discussion of God up until this point. His previous encounters as described by Phillip had left him jaded, or at least that's what she'd assumed. "What do you mean no?"

"God is not responsible for what happened."

"What..."

Duncan put up his hand to stop her. "I'm not an expert on God; but the little I know leads me to believe He cares about people, right?"

She made no reply. The crunch of the dirt and grass beneath the horses' hooves filled the silence. Duncan began again. "At least that's what I understand. That means no matter what happened, He still cares about you, right?"

"If he did, then my father wouldn't have died, and my mother wouldn't have locked herself away from the world for all these years."

Duncan had nothing to add to that, but he still had one question left. "But, why does that mean you don't deserve someone like Sophia has to care about her?"

Helen clenched her teeth and barely bit out an answer. "Because if God doesn't even care about me, why should anyone else?"

She clicked to her horse and forced it to move ahead of Duncan, coming alongside the sulking Phillip. Duncan could feel something he'd never felt before, his heart breaking for someone else. She was so broken, just like him. He wanted to fix that brokenness inside her, somehow. If only she'd let him.

"I think you deserve it," he whispered.

Phillip barely acknowledged Helen's presence beside him. She seemed content to let him wallow in his own worries. For once, he appreciated her moody demeanor.

He didn't understand what Duncan was up to. What was the value in making Jacob think they trusted him, when clearly they didn't? How was that going to help anything? It just didn't make any sense.

And meanwhile, Sophia was out there somewhere. Who knows what was happening to her right at this moment?

"You thinking about her?"

Her quiet voice startled him. Had Helen ever spoken so quietly before? "Yes. I'm worried about her. Worried we won't find her in time before something bad happens to her." He didn't know what else to say and so stopped talking.

"Me too."

He glanced over at her. Her face was still as hard as stone, but he could see her struggling to remain that way. "It's okay to be worried about her. She is your cousin after all. I won't judge you if you start crying or something." Again, he wasn't sure what to say; so, he stopped.

She shook her head. "I don't cry, but I appreciate the offer. You and your friend…" She briefly made eye contact before looking at the ground again. "I'm glad that Sophia and I ran into you in the woods. I'm glad you're here."

"It's getting dark."

Both Helen and Phillip glanced forward, seeing Jacob turning his horse around to face them. "I say we should settle down for the night. Since we've been moving at a good pace today, we should be able to catch up with them tomorrow. That is, as long as I don't lose the trail again." His smile was a weak one, and not appreciated in Phillip's opinion.

"Fine. But tomorrow we ride without stopping, no excuses." He quickly dismounted and tied his horse to a nearby tree. There was no stream close, so they would have to rely on the water they brought with them for the moment.

"You know I'm trying to help, right? You don't have to keep acting like you don't trust me."

Jacob's voice suddenly coming from behind him startled him; and he put his hand on his sword without thinking. He watched the man's eyes dart down to follow his movement and then move back up to meet his own gaze. Part of him wanted to trust the man, but a stronger part of him was convinced he was somehow responsible for Sophia's kidnapping.

"Truce? You don't really have to trust me; but if you at least pretend it won't make this so hard."

Phillip shook his head at the ridiculous idea. "Just stay out of my way."

He shoved past him and stepped further into the forest. "I need a few minutes alone."

Sophia collapsed in the dirt, barely able to catch herself from completely falling on her face and scraping it up in the process. She felt the palms of her hands slap the ground and her wrists snap back painfully as she tried to brace herself. Her knees gave out; and she lay half huddled on the ground, straining for breath and squeezing her eyes shut to block out the tears that continued to threaten her cheeks.

"Did I say stop?"

He kicked her in the side, not hard enough to cause any permanent damage, but hard enough to leave a bruise. She continued to choke on the gag as she strove for a deep breath. Some of the knots behind her head loosened, and she felt the gag slip free. Before she could stop herself, she was choking and gagging trying to keep from throwing up on the ground.

"Here." She felt the canteen hit her head and fall to the ground, just next to her bound hands. "Drink slowly. Don't want to have to clean up after you."

Sophia did as she was told, grasping the canteen with both hands and taking small sips of water. Eventually, her stomach stopped tumbling; and she felt she could stand up again. To that end, she carefully shuffled to her feet, still taking time to breathe deeply through her mouth.

Her kidnapper grunted and tugged on her leash, pulling her forward abruptly and almost causing her to tumble to her feet again. Her long skirt tangled around her ankles and tripped her up. To her surprise, they only went a short distance before she felt her back being shoved against a tree and ropes once again being tied around her chest and stomach. *Does he have an infinite amount of rope, or does he keep reusing the same rope over and over? If the latter is true, that means he's not cutting the rope; he's untying the knots each time. That must mean that the knots are not all that strong!* She wriggled a bit to test her theory.

Slap! The palm of a hand crashed across the side of her face, snapping her neck to one side.

"Don't be trying to escape! Didn't I already explain what the consequences for that were? Do you need a reminder?"

The image of the knife blade pressed to her throat was all she needed. Sophia shook her head, resigned to her fate for the moment. The ropes wrapped once again around her ankles, tighter than she remembered from before. *At least I won't have to worry about falling down, he's got these ropes tied so tight I won't move at all, even if I can't support myself anymore.*

She was thoroughly exhausted by the time her kidnapper left her alone for the night. Her stomach growled, and Sophia suddenly realized that not only had she not eaten that day; but her kidnapper had not replaced the gag in her mouth. She bit her lip self-consciously. Perhaps as long as she stayed quiet, he wouldn't put it back in. *It'll certainly make breathing easier. I can barely breathe through my nose with this stupid blindfold covering half my face.*

It was with this thought uppermost in her mind that she drifted off to sleep.

The crackling of the fire, that Jacob had insisted they start "since the nights were getting chillier each day" according to him, was not what kept Phillip awake that night. Helen had taken first watch but had been relieved by Jacob about an hour ago. The fire did manage to keep away the bugs, so the night was rather quiet. That was why Phillip could hear when Jacob got up from his place at the fire and started rifling through his pack. Trying to lay as still as possible, to make it seem like he was still asleep, Phillip strained his ears to continue to hear the movement. He heard the rustling stop first. Then he heard the footsteps. Cautiously, he rolled over, still trying to pretend like it was just movement in his sleep. He even threw in a loud sigh for effect. He heard the movement stop right after his dramatic input, but only for a moment. Clearly, when Jacob felt satisfied that Phillip was still asleep, he continued with whatever he was doing in the middle of the night.

When the footsteps had almost faded away from his hearing, Phillip threw off his blanket and grabbed his sword lying beside him. He decided not to wake Helen or Duncan just in case he was wrong. *No need to get them involved unless there's a reason.* In the back of his mind, he could still remember Helen's concerns about someone following them. She hadn't mentioned that for a while. *Perhaps because the one who was following us is now with us?* He shivered and hurriedly followed Jacob further into the forest. He tried to focus on remaining as silent as possible, but Jacob was moving quickly, as if he knew exactly where he was headed, and soon was out of Phillip's range of vision. He stopped to regroup for a moment.

Glancing back, he saw that they were probably about a good fifteen to twenty minutes' walk from where they'd camped for the night. *Of course, we've been running, so I've only been gone about five to ten minutes. Maybe I could track him if I...*

Thunk!

Phillip had heard nothing before the sudden assault. Something hit him over the back of the head, and he fell with a *thud*. He reached to withdraw his sword, but a boot slammed down on his hand and he let out a short yell. Before he could move again, the same boot smashed into his face. He collapsed into the grass and slipped into unconsciousness.

Chapter Thirteen

Sophia heard the footsteps while she was still half asleep. Forcing herself awake, she listened as they moved behind her tree. *Probably not right behind my tree; but somewhere close enough that I can hear them moving. They can't be more than ten, maybe fifteen feet away.* She held her breath, but they never came around to the front of the tree.

"Why have you come?" she heard the raspy voice speak first.

The other voice was quiet, like it was unsure of who could possibly hear them in an abandoned forest. "You don't have to do this. Just take her back. The others…"

"Are weak! I don't care about what they do. They won't interfere. You'll make sure they don't. That was our deal."

The other voice didn't say anything for a few moments. "It doesn't have to be this way. She didn't do anything to you."

"But she must pay for what was done to me."

Pay? She felt that panicking lump making a return in her throat. Her chest constricted as she tried to keep her breathing quiet. It didn't seem like a good idea to let them know that she'd heard them talking.

They continued talking for a few minutes, but it must have been too quiet for her to hear, or they'd moved further away from her tree. It didn't matter.

God, where are you? I'm so afraid.

You are not alone, Sophia.

She felt her breathing ease for a moment. She'd heard this voice before. This still, small comforting voice.

But, I'm afraid.

Do not fear. I am with you.

It doesn't feel like it.

That doesn't make it any less true.

"Then rescue me," she whispered, not sure if she cared if raspy voice heard her or not. "Get me out of here."

There was no response to her request. But, the lump of panic had dissolved and replaced itself with a warm feeling that spread throughout her body. She slipped back to sleep as the night wind whipped around her, making the warmth in her heart feel that much more real.

"Phillip? Phillip, can you hear me?"

The voice calling him back to consciousness sounded desperate. Why were they so worried? Why couldn't they just let him sleep for five more...

Slap!

He shot up instantly, rubbing his hand against his cheek where he could feel it blushing red from the offending smack. "What was that for?" He shook his head to clear his blurry vision.

Jacob knelt next to him, rubbing his right hand on his leg. "Have you got a rock for a head or what?" He smiled in what appeared to be genuine relief.

Phillip glanced around him. He couldn't figure out where he was for a few moments. Then it all came back to him in a rush. One look at the moon told him it was about an hour after he had initially followed Jacob from the campground.

"Where did you go off to? You were supposed to be keeping watch?"

He shrugged. "I walked around the perimeter, checking it out. I must have gone back to the campgrounds a different way or I would have found you sooner. When I realized you were gone, I came back out to look for you." He smiled. "Don't worry, I woke Duncan up to keep an eye on the camp while I came back out."

Sounds like a plausible explanation. But then... "Someone knocked me out."

A frown furrowed across Jacob's face. "Did you see who?"

121

No, but I have my suspicions. "Of course not. It was dark, and he came up behind me. He hit me in the back of the head with something, stepped on my hand, and then kicked me in the face." He rubbed his chin, feeling the tender beginnings of a bruise there.

"Hm," Jacob replied, seeming to be thinking about something else entirely. "We should probably keep moving then. I know it's not quite light out, but it will be soon enough." He pointed off to their left. "I picked up the trail heading that direction. If we move quickly, we should be able to catch up with them by the end of the day."

Seems real enough. "Yes, let's get going. Since Duncan's already awake, I'll let him wake up Helen." A smirk traced his face. "We can be on the road within the hour?"

Jacob nodded and held out his hand to help Phillip up off the ground. The beginnings of a headache pierced his skull as he accepted the help and stood to his feet. He dusted off his clothes with a sweep of his hands. A sideways glance showed Jacob still patiently waiting for him before returning to camp. *Maybe he's not so bad after all. Maybe...maybe he really didn't have anything to do with Sophia's kidnapping.*

The two walked silently back to camp as these thoughts continues to stream through Phillip's mind.

"Get up!"

The raspy voice pierced through her sleeping mind and she struggled to pull herself from her deep sleep. Sophia shook her head from side to side, trying desperately to wake up. She could feel the ropes around her chest loosening again, and the ropes around her ankles had already been untied. She tumbled forward and caught herself with her hands. He obviously hadn't tied the additional rope around her wrists yet. "Water?" she heard herself whisper. Her voice was almost as raspy as him; she was completely parched. She licked her dry and cracked lips, but there was no moisture to give them.

"Here," she heard him growl. The canteen tumbled towards her, and she scrambled for it. "Take this too." Just as she grabbed hold of the canteen, another loaf of bread like he'd given her before brushed against her hand. "Eat it and hurry up. We've got to get moving."

Eagerly, Sophia drank half the canteen before starting on the loaf of bread. She was long past hunger, and the bread felt like rocks as it dropped into her stomach. It was enough to make her nauseous, but she easily finished the canteen in spite of her discomfort.

"Good," the raspy voice said, snatching the canteen from her hands as soon as she'd finished the last drops of water. She felt him attach the "leash" from the previous day and yanked her off the ground. Her shoulders felt as though they would break right from the rest of her body as they started moving forward. Her feet, still half asleep and swollen, struggled to move with her kidnapper.

"Give me a moment!" she finally said, exasperated, tugging at the leash. To her surprise, the tension released; and she felt some slack in the rope. She straightened herself up, stretching her legs one at a time. She finally felt her mind clearing from sleep and starting to become more and more alert. It occurred to her that he still hadn't replaced her gag. "No gag today?"

"Don't make me regret it. Are you ready to keep moving, *your highness?*" he replied, lacing each of his words with sarcasm. She could almost imagine him faking a curtsy with his words. *I wish I could see him. I'm never going to escape if I don't even know what I'm up against...I suppose it's good that I'm at least thinking about escaping, no matter how much of a long-shot that might be.*

She held out her hands and took a step forward, trying to show that she was ready to comply. Without another word, they were off: Sophia being dragged through the forest, and her kidnapper leading the way. It was then that she noticed there were still crickets chirping. *It has to still be nighttime. Why are we moving now so suddenly? What's changed?* Then she remembered the conversation she'd overheard last night...*or was it earlier tonight? I wish I knew what time it was!* Her mind was more alert than it had been since she'd been kidnapped. She could feel options clicking through her brain, abandoning each one as it shifted through. At the moment, there weren't really any options, unfortunately.

A tree branch slapped her in the face, and she cried out, feeling the scrape on her cheek starting to bleed. "I don't suppose you could remove this blindfold, so I could see where I'm going?" She smiled internally. *That almost sounded brave.*

"And give you information that you could use to help yourself escape? Not a chance." He snickered. "You'll just have to trust me." He snickered again, tugged on her leash, and moved faster through the forest.

Sophia sighed. She could feel the ropes chafing her wrists, and she had no interest in speeding up that process. Pushing herself to move faster helped to loosen the tension and give herself some slack to work with. Small pebbles worked their way into her shoe, and she struggled to kick them out while continuing to move.

As the air around her grew warmer, she figured the sun must have finally decided to rise. *How long have we been walking? I wonder how far we've gotten.* She remembered again the conversation from earlier. *Should I ask him about it? He probably won't answer me anyway. But that lets me know that he's got at least one person working with him. Does he have anyone else? He mentioned "the others".* She gasped. *Could that mean Phillip and Helen and Duncan? Where are they? They must be nearby! That must be why we're moving again, trying to get further away from them.* She felt that warm feeling spreading through her again. *They're coming to rescue me! I'm going to be rescued!*

I told you not to be afraid.

The voice startled her.

"Thank you," she whispered.

"What was that?" the raspy voice snapped.

"Nothing," she replied. "Pardon me for thinking out loud."

"Just don't do it again, or I'll have to put that gag back on."

She smiled, hoping he wasn't looking at her. Apparently, he wasn't since he didn't comment further. *I'm not afraid of you. I'm going to be rescued.*

Sophia was exhausted when they finally stopped. They'd been walking for hours, the entire day in fact. He'd only allowed brief rests once or twice throughout the day. She collapsed entirely to the ground, panting and burying her face in her hands to hide her tears of relief. *I'm not afraid of you. I'm going to be rescued.* The twin thoughts had become her mantra, repeated over and over in her mind throughout the day. She continued to repeat them as he tied her back to another tree, retied the rope around her ankles, and finally replaced the gag in her mouth.

"Can't risk having you make any noise tonight" was the only comment she got from her kidnapper. *That means they must be closer than he wants! He's worried I might cry out, and they'd hear me. They've got to be close!*

She fell asleep with that hope in her heart, singing her to sleep with its sweet song.

"We have to move now!"

"We should wait until morning. It will be easier to see then."

"He'll probably move her again in the morning! That's why we have to go now," Phillip let out a groan of frustration. *Just when I'd started to like this guy...* "Helen, you say something. It's your cousin!"

She shot him a glare, reminding him that even though she'd softened up...there was still quite a bit of the old Helen left behind. Then she rolled her eyes and turned to Jacob. "He has a point. If you're sure she's so close, there's not really a reason to wait until tomorrow."

Jacob let out a sigh of frustration. "We'd don't know enough. Who kidnapped her? How many are there? What kind of weapons do they have? What's the setup of their camp? These are questions that need answers before we charge in foolishly."

Duncan stepped in the middle of the group with his hands spread, as though attempting to calm their emotions with a wave of his hands. "Enough," he shot a look at Phillip as he turned to face the opposite direction. "Jacob, since you seem confident that you've figured out her location, why don't you spend tonight scoping it out? Find out the answers to all those pesky questions."

Jacob nodded his assent. He turned away from the rest of them, tying his horse to a tree and then heading out on foot in the direction he'd pointed out earlier.

Helen folded her arms across her chest. "What was that? Whose side are you on anyway? There's four of us. If whoever this kidnapper is had more than that, he wouldn't be moving so quickly through the forest. Simple fact."

"I know that." Duncan picked up the reigns she'd dropped partway through the argument and tied both their horses off.

Helen and Phillip exchanged a look before he spoke, "Then…"

"You should follow him and see where he goes." Duncan looked at them both very calmly, meeting Phillip's confused stare head-on.

"Follow him?"

"Look," Duncan said with a sigh, "we don't trust him. And after that suspicious incident last night, I see no reason to beat around the bush any longer. If we do," here he paused for a moment to look at Helen with concern in his eyes, "someone could be seriously hurt. It'd be a better idea to let him think I still trust him, while also finding out where he's going. If the opportunity opens up to rescue Sophia in the process, you" here he glanced at Phillip, "you take that chance. Come and get us if you need to."

Finally understanding, Phillip handed his reigns to Duncan, put his hand on his sword, and followed Jacob into the forest.

Chapter Fourteen

The footsteps woke her first. *It must be that other person, coming back to meet again. I've got to hear what he has to say!* She strained her ears to hear the first hint of conversation that might come. To her surprise, she didn't hear any voices, only footsteps coming closer and closer. She felt her heart begin to race faster and faster as they approached. They were moving with confidence, not worried about being heard. She wanted to cry out but remembered the gag had been replaced in her mouth. Sophia strained against the ropes. *If it were the kidnapper, he would have said something by now.* The panic that she'd thought she'd conquered tried to make a comeback. *I'm not afraid. I'm going to be rescued.* The words sounded empty and hollow as the fear crowded out all other emotions. Her breath came in short spurts. In-out-in-out, faster and faster the closer the footsteps came.

Then they stopped. She knew they had to be right behind her tree. *I will not cry. I will not let them see me cry! God, where are you? You said you were with me. Where are you now?*

"Sophia?"

The voice startled her completely. "Hmhm?" Her question was muffled by the gag, but she was so shocked she seemed incapable of doing anything else.

"Hold on; I'm going to untie you. Then I'll get the gag, okay?"

She nodded, still completely in shock.

The now familiar feeling of ropes loosening around first her ankles, and then her chest. Then, she felt the knots around her hands come loose for the first time in…*Three days? Has it only been three days, now? It feels like a lifetime.*

Her wrists ached, and she rubbed them self-consciously as her rescuer untied first the gag and then finally the blindfold.

"Jacob?" Her voice was light and hoarse from lack of use. She was thirsty again. "Do you have any water?"

A relieved smile covered his face. "Yes, I've got some. Here," he said, handing her a freshly filled canteen. She drank eagerly, letting some of the water dribble down her chin in her haste.

"Whoa! Slow down or you'll choke," he whispered. She responded by handing the canteen back, significantly lighter than it was before. "Ready to get out of here?"

"Where is everyone else? Are Phillip and…"

"Yes, they're with me. They've made camp a little way away. I came ahead to scout things out and found you alone. Figured it was good timing for a getaway."

"Good timing, yes; but not exactly for a getaway."

The owner of the raspy voice had seemingly appeared out of nowhere, emerging from the night like a ghost. This was the first time Sophia was actually looking at him face to face, and it was quite a surprise. *I'm not sure what I was expecting with those wrinkled hands and that raspy voice.*

Her kidnapper was only slightly taller than her. While he looked strong, with well-toned muscles in his arms and legs; he was clearly older, probably close to fifty or sixty. His head was covered with a mess of untidy gray hair that looked like it hadn't been washed or combed in weeks. In his hand, he held a sword…her mother's sword, to her surprise! *Does he know what it can do? How could he know that?*

"I'm surprised at you, Jacob."

"You know him?" Sophia glanced at Jacob with surprise and a touch of disappointment in her voice. She'd wanted to believe the best about everyone in the village, but now… "Were you the one who was following us? Who attacked Helen?"

Jacob wasn't looking at her, didn't even acknowledge that he'd heard her. His eyes were locked on her kidnapper. A bead of sweat was running down the side of his face although there was still a chill in the night air.

"Alone in the forest with an impressionable, young lady? What will your wife say?"

Sophia inched towards Jacob, still slightly unsteady on her feet. She reached out her hand to touch his arm, but then drew back. "Jacob, what is he talking about? How does he know you're married?"

There was still no response from the stone statue named Jacob. But drops of sweating were exploding into existence all across his face.

"You should say hello to her for me. Say hello to your wife…and my grandson." He snickered and looked to Sophia for her reaction.

"Grandson?" she stuttered. The blood drained from her face. "Jacob?" she said, turning to him for a response.

He didn't face her. Didn't break his gaze from her kidnapper. When he spoke, it wasn't addressed to her. "Leave her out of this. She didn't do anything to you."

"Didn't do anything to me?" His voice shook from the restrained emotion. The sword in his hand started to slowly move forward. "She took everything from me! Everything! I am an outcast because of her!"

"I don't even know you!" Sophia cried out. "I've never met you before in my life!"

Her kidnapper continued speaking in a sort of low mutter, not directly addressed at her; but it appeared he was choosing to still speak loud enough for her to hear him. "First her father, then her, and now her daughter. They just keep coming back. Their lives just keep getting better and better, while my life keeps getting worse and worse. They've taken my army, my kingdom, my son…"

"Your son?!" Sophia gasped, looking at Jacob. *What was he talking about "her father" and "her daughter"? Did this crazy guy know Mother?!*

Jacob finally moved forward with his hand stretched out to placate the old man. "Please don't do this. You haven't lost me, but you will if you don't let her go right now."

Sophia was still completely confused. *Jacob is his son? Does that mean that he helped his father with the kidnapping, or he didn't know anything about it? And...* "How do you know my mother?"

"She took it all away. It was here," the old man held out one wrinkled hand, the one that wasn't holding the sword. "And she took it from me!" He made his hand into a fist and continued ignoring Sophia for the moment. "She took the life I wanted, the life I deserved..." He locked eyes with Jacob and said fiercely. "The life you deserved."

"I'm fine with my life! All I wanted was you!" Jacob insisted. "Please, just let us go."

"Never! I can still take her life. Her hopes and dreams wrapped up in her child. I can take this one to pay for what was taken from me."

What is he saying? Is he actually going to kill me? "What did you do, Mother?" Sophia whispered under her breath.

"You can't kill her, Father," Jacob said, an edge to his voice. "Just let us leave, and everything will be fine."

"You say I haven't lost you, but you would choose *her* over me."

Jacob's eyes widened. "That's not what this is! It's just not right for you to take Sophia's life for something she didn't do. It's not her fault."

"You have a choice, Jacob." The old man casually tossed Sophia's sword to the ground in front of Jacob's feet. "You can either kill her, in payment for what was done to me; or you can kill me to stop me forever." He paused, making sure that Jacob understood the seriousness of the matter before him. "But understand, if you don't kill me now; I will find her again. This will never be over until one of us is dead."

Sophia watched in silent horror as the blood drained from Jacob's face. There were tears in his eyes as he spoke next, "Father, please. You don't have to do this. She didn't do anything to you."

You don't have to do this. She didn't do anything to you. That voice. Those words. She gasped as the pieces fell into place. *That was Jacob I heard the other night? What was the "deal" they* *spoke of? He <u>was</u> a part of this all along! How could he betray us like that?*

Jacob's hands were shaking as he picked up the sword his father had dropped in front of him. He looked at Sophia and then back at his father. The tears were flowing freely now. *He looks like a frightened child. Please, God. Help me...help Jacob!*

Thunk!

The old man crumbled to the ground with a low moan.

"Phillip!" Sophia cried out, rushing past Jacob towards him. He held his sword in one hand, replacing it in his sheath with a shake of his head. She threw her arms around him, burying her face in his shoulder. "You got here just in time."

He pulled back at first, startled by her emotionally charged reaction to him. Then, he relaxed and returned the embrace, a blush coloring his cheeks. "I'm glad I made it." He glanced at the crumpled form on the ground. "I hope I didn't hurt the old guy. I just meant to knock him out, but I guess I hit him a little harder than I intended."

Sophia pulled away and glanced at her kidnapper. *He certainly doesn't look as menacing when he's unconscious.*

It was then that she remembered Jacob. He was standing, staring at the crumpled form of his father with tears still streaming down his face. Her sword was still gripped loosely in his hand.

Slowly, she pulled away from Phillip and moved towards Jacob. She gently took her sword from his grasp and paused for a moment, taking the situation in without speaking. "Thank you for rescuing me, or trying to anyway," she finally said.

His eyes were filled to the brim with tears as he looked away from his father lying on the ground. "I'm so sorry for what he did, what he tried to do." He looked away from her. "I never would have hurt you. I want you to know that. This wasn't what was supposed to happen."

"Sophia?" Both her and Jacob turned their attention to Phillip, who was still standing a few feet away from the still form of her kidnapper. "What is he talking about? What does he mean 'he never would hurt you'?"

131

"Phillip…" She walked toward him, grabbing his arm and starting to pull him away. "Let's just get going, okay?"

"No," he said, shoving off her arm and looking quickly between her and Jacob. "I demand to know what is going on. I'm the one who rescued you!" He shot a glare in Jacob's direction. "I have no idea what he was trying to do."

Jacob looked at Sophia, eyes filled with a mixture of hopelessness and relief. Hopeless of hiding the truth any longer, and relief that he would no longer have to carry that burden. He nodded his head briefly, giving her permission to tell what she knew.

"Phillip," she gestured to the crazed kidnapper lying at their feet, "this is Jacob's father."

"His…father?!" Before Sophia could say another word, Phillip's sword was in his hand and pointed at Jacob's throat. "You knew! You knew who did this, and you *helped him*, didn't you? It's a good thing Duncan had me follow you, or I may never have gotten her back!"

"Phillip, calm down!"

"So, Duncan told you to follow me? I guess no one trusted me…not even my father."

"Why on earth would we trust you? I was right about everything!"

"Phillip, don't hurt him!"

A pinprick of blood appeared on Jacob's throat. "Just tell me this, why did you do all this? Why did he, your *father*, do all this? What was the point?"

"Revenge," Jacob said quietly. "He wanted revenge. I wanted no part in it, but…" He looked up at Sophia, looking past Philip to lock his gaze with hers. "But, he's my father. What could I do?"

A moaning sound interrupted their conversation. All three turned their attention to the formerly unconscious figure on the ground. Slowly, but surely, he was starting to return to consciousness. Phillip moved quickly to retrieve the discarded rope and gag that Jacob had dropped by Sophia's tree. He quickly bound his hands

132

behind his back and placed the gag in his mouth. Sophia's heart ached a little to see an elderly man treated in such a manner. *But, what else can we do? He was going to kill me.*

Surprisingly, Jacob did not protest Philip's actions. He still seemed stuck in a sort of shock impenetrable by normal interactions. *I don't know what to do, God. I don't know how to help him.* She placed one hand gently on his arm, trying to provide some reassurance.

"Now what?" Phillip said. He stood looking at his handiwork as he spoke. The kidnapper had not yet fully regained consciousness, but he soon would. The three of them stood silently taking in the situation, unsure of how to proceed. It was Sophia who spoke next.

"We can't leave him here, can we?" She looked at Jacob as she spoke.

"We can't take him with us," Phillip argued, "and I'm not leaving him" with a glance at Jacob "here unsupervised. Not after everything that's happened."

Jacob nodded. "I would do the same." He looked at Sophia with a look of resignation. "He's a lot more resourceful than you might think. Those ropes won't hold him for long, so we'd best get moving. He'll pick up our trail and be after us as soon as he's able."

Sophia and Phillip exchanged concerned looks, but it seemed like there was no better option at the moment. "I can't kill him, Phillip. He's just an old man, after all." She looked down at the sword in the scabbard at her side. *Am I doing the right thing, God? He said he'd come after me. I don't want to spend the rest of my life running.*

Do not be afraid. I am with you.

"I'm going to have to tie him up too, Sophia." He looked almost apologetically at her as he used the remaining ropes to bind Jacob's hands. He looked like a lamb being led to the slaughter as the three of them made their way back to through the forest to the camp. The rain started when they were halfway back.

She sat staring out the window as the rain beat down, pounding the grass flat with a vengeance. The sound was rather soothing to her tired soul.

"Katherine?"

Michael's head appeared in the doorway with a plate of food in one hand. He entered the bedroom quietly, setting the plate down on the bed as he went to stand beside her at the window.

"I hope she's staying warm enough." Katherine laughed. "Isn't it silly? Of all the things I could be worried about, that's the fear running through my mind." She looked out the window and watched the rain as she continued speaking. "Do you remember how when she was little she used to run around outside whenever it rained? She'd jump in all the puddles and splash Solomon when she could convince him to come out with her. He always hated getting wet." Her gaze shifted to the ground as tears filled her eyes. "She'd always come back inside, cold and soaking wet. The servants were always in such a tizzy to get her warmed up before she started sneezing."

She buried her face in her hands as the tears started to fall like the raindrops outside her window, pounding down relentlessly. "Michael, who's going to take care of her while she's out there? Helen was never good at that kind of thing…"

His hands wrapped around her waist in a gentle embrace and pulled her close. She turned away from the window and sobbed into his shoulder, his hands stroking her back in an effort to calm her fried nerves. After a few moments, she pulled away from him, leaving her hands in his as a last piece of warmth against the cold fear stealing through her heart.

"Hey, where is this sudden display of motherly affection coming from?" Michael teased. "The last time you were this weepy over something as small as a rain shower was when you were pregnant with Solomon." He gave her a quick sideways glance. "There's not something you need to tell me, is there?"

"Of course not!" Katherine pulled her hands away and crossed her arms, a mock pout on her face. "I'm simply worried about our *daughter*, out in the world with that madman following her!"

He scowled. "You don't know that, Katherine. It was a dream. A bad dream, to be sure; but it doesn't tell you anything about who is really following Sophia and Helen."

"But I feel it," she argued. "Doesn't that count for something? We never caught him, Michael. We know he can hold a grudge. It would be entirely possible for him to…"

"To what? Follow a pair of girls traveling alone on the off chance that one of them is your daughter?" Michael shook his head. "If he'd wanted to do something like that, he would have tried a long time ago. Why wait this long?"

Katherine went and sat on the edge of the bed, toying with the fork on the tray he'd carried in. "I just can't put it out of my mind that easily. I've continued to have that dream every night since Edwin returned."

He moved around to the side of the bed, kneeling in front of her and grasping her shaking hands in her lap. "Katherine, why didn't you tell me?"

She wouldn't look him in the eye. "What was I supposed to say?"

For a long time, neither of them spoke. The rain beat down on the sides of the castle walls, and streaks of lightning flashed through the sky. Michael finally moved from his kneeling position to sit on the bed beside his wife. She leaned her head against his shoulder, wiping a hand across her face to catch the remaining tears.

"Katherine," Michael finally asked, "have you heard from Lilly recently?"

Slowly, she sat up and turned to face him, puzzled expression firmly in place. "Have I heard from Lilly recently? No, probably not since last summer."

"Hmm."

"Michael, what are you up to?"

He smiled. "Nothing, I just thought perhaps it might be nice to pay a visit to an old friend, living in the village where we first met…" He winked. "It's supposed to be nicer weather that far south in the kingdom, yes?"

Realization and understanding flooded Katherine and sent her heart leaping into her chest. She threw her arms around him, knocking him backwards onto the bed, and knocking the tray of food onto the floor in the process with a loud *clang*. "Thank you, Michael! Thank you! I don't know why I didn't think of it before!"

He let out a genuine laugh. "That's why they let me make decisions around here, on occasion anyway. But look at what a mess you've made! I just can't take you anywhere!"

They were both laughing so hard; they didn't hear the door open with a quiet knock. Solomon poked his head into the room first, followed by the rest of his body when he heard the laugher. "What's so funny?"

The king and queen sat up suddenly, with tears still streaming down Michael's face from laughing so hard. Katherine's smile dropped when she glanced at Solomon. "You're soaking wet!" She jumped up from the bed, grabbing a blanket from the chair where she'd been sitting earlier, and wrapping it around him. Gently, she moved damp pieces of hair out of his eyes.

"Mother…" he pulled away from her, but accepted the blanket, wrapping it around his shoulders and shivering slightly.

Katherine and Michael exchanged a meaningful look as she stepped back. "What did you need, Solomon?"

"I just came from the church." He stepped past Katherine and faced Michael with what he hoped was a brave stance, at least to the best of a sixteen-year-old's ability. "Father, I want to ask permission to go after Sophia. I feel there's something wrong, and I can't sit here waiting any longer." He looked down at the ground, the bulk of his message having been delivered. "She's my sister, after all."

As she was behind Solomon so her facial expressions were unseen, she felt safe cracking a smile. Here was her son, trying to be so grown up; but he was standing here soaking wet, wrapped in a blanket, like the little boy she remembered comforting on her lap during many a previous rainstorm.

The irony was not lost on Michael either, although he had to fight his smile since Solomon was looking at him eagerly awaiting an answer. "Actually, your mother and I were just discussing a trip to the southern part of the kingdom. Do you remember your mother's young friend Lilly from when you were a child?"

Solomon thought for a moment, obviously trying to recall the possible connection to their current situation. "Um…"

"It's okay, you were rather young," Katherine interrupted. "She's married now and living in the same village where your father and I met in the southern part of the kingdom. Perhaps you'd like to come with us?"

His cheeky half smile flashed across his face, and she could tell that Solomon was having a hard time containing his joy.

"Why don't you go tell Edwin our plans? I think it would be best if we traveled lightly, so you, your mother and I will travel with just two of his men. Tell him he may choose who accompanies us, but I'd like him to remain here with Adam to look after the castle. I'd like to leave tomorrow morning if at all possible."

Solomon nodded and headed towards the door. Suddenly remembering that he was wrapped in a blanket long enough to cause him to trip, he sheepishly handed the sopping wet blanket to his mother. His clothes weren't dripping quite as bad anymore, but his hair still had droplets of water ready to fall at any moment. Katherine received the blanket from him and smiled. "Put on some dry clothes first, please. No reason to catch a cold."

He nodded again and rushed out of the room, pulling the door shut behind him.

Chapter Fifteen

"Now what?" Helen said haughtily. "Why'd you bring him back here?" She crossed her arms and glared angrily at Phillip. When he and Sophia had returned bearing a captive Jacob in tow, she hadn't been too surprised. She'd never trusted the falsely hospitable man to begin with. They'd left Jacob sitting tied up a little way away from the camp with the horses; surprisingly, he hadn't tried to escape yet. It wasn't like they were doing an incredible job of watching him, since the four of them had been standing around arguing since then.

"What would you suggest? Since you always seem to have all the answers," Phillip shot back. Sophia hadn't said a word to contribute to the discussion since she'd explained what had happened from her perspective. Instead, she sat staring into the remains of the fire completely lost in thought. Helen felt a twinge of worry trying to make its way to the surface. *What did he do to her?*

Duncan put up his hand to stop the argument. "Whatever we decide, we need to be on the move soon. His father won't stop just because he's lost his prisoner. Revenge is a powerful motivator, especially if he's held this grudge for over eighteen years already. Perhaps we should take Jacob back to the village, let them handle a suitable punishment?"

"Please! Please don't!" The weak cry startled them, and they all turned to face Jacob, except Sophia who continued to stare into the dead fire.

Tears were flowing unrestrained down his face, and his voice cracked as he spoke. "I can't face them. My wife, my son…" He hung his head in shame. "They never knew about my family's horrible past. As far as she knows, my father was crazy and disappeared many months ago. Lilly will have told her that I followed after Sophia and her kidnapper. I can't return home as an assistant to that kidnapping." Overcome by emotion, he struggled to finish his thought, "I can't return home such a disappointment to my family."

Unsure what to make of his story, Helen cleared her throat. "Perhaps we could just take him with us for right now? We're almost to the border of Suffrom. Taking me there gives him the time to figure out how to deal with his family when he goes back. Then the rest of you can take him back to the village." She uncrossed her arms and placed her right hand on her hip, leaving her left resting on her sword hilt. "Everyone wins."

"You can't go alone into Suffrom. We can't just leave you at the border," Sophia said softly. She finally raised her head to meet the eyes of her friends. "Someone has to go with you."

"Not going to convince me to go back to the castle again?"

Sophia shook her head. "It wouldn't make a difference, would it?"

"No," Helen acknowledged. "But no one has to go with me. I'll be fine."

"I will."

She snapped her head to her right to acknowledge Duncan's statement. His eyes seemed determined, but the rest of him seemed completely at ease. Helen searched for a reason to dismiss him but found none. Surprisingly, she felt a wave of relief wash over her. "Alright," she finally said. "I guess a guard to accompany me wouldn't be so bad."

He nodded, as Phillip protested, "But you can't just run away from all of this, Helen! And Duncan, you can't give up your life here…"

"What life? I have no family left, and you're my only friend. Perhaps," he paused. "Perhaps this was God's plan all along."

Phillip scoffed. "God's plan? I thought you didn't believe in God."

"Perhaps not," a shrug, "but perhaps it makes more sense than I'd like to admit." All five were silent, without an appropriate response to this statement.

"Then it's settled," Helen said, the first to break up the group as she headed towards her horse. "We'll head to the border of Suffrom; it shouldn't take more than a few days."

139

The first day passed mostly in silence, everyone lost in their own thoughts.

Jacob's heart hurt with every beat, it reminded him of the shame brought on by his father coursing through his blood. What would his wife say when he returned? How could he ever admit to her that he had assisted in Princess Sophia's kidnapping? What kind of father could he ever hope to become with the type of example he'd been brought up with?

Duncan's musings were mostly related to God. It wasn't really that he didn't believe in God, rather he'd been indifferent for most of his life. His life had been filled with both good and bad things, but so wasn't everyone's life? But since he had met Helen and Sophia, hearing Sophia speak about the One True God like he was a real person, and with the feelings that were growing stronger each day for Helen…perhaps it was time to give God a chance.

Helen, per usual, was perfectly content with the silence. Mixed emotions rolled inside her like a boiling sea. She was so close to her homeland, her birthplace, but she felt like she was stepping off a cliff and falling into the unknown. It was easy to dismiss the feelings of isolation over the last few weeks being constantly surrounded by people, even annoying ones like Phillip. But as the prospect of heading over the border and finishing the rest of her journey quite separated from all the familiar loomed in the near future, she was secretly glad that Duncan had insisted on joining her.

Phillip, for once, couldn't find the words to express everything that was going on inside him. He struggled to understand Duncan's sudden interest in the spiritual. What was he thinking? Didn't he know that religion couldn't be trusted? That God didn't exist, or if he did didn't care about them? And now, now he was going to leave him…for Helen. And while he was happy that his friend had found someone to care for in that way, it left him feeling left out. It was clear Sophia felt nothing for him; so, when all this was over he would be alone, again.

Sophia rode at the tail end of the group, barely keeping pace with the rest of the horses. She couldn't get the words of that madman out of her head. What had Mother done to him that deserved such hatred? Perhaps she should have killed him; now she could only hope to outrun him. But could she keep running for the rest of her life? And where was God in all of this? He had felt so real to her during the past few days, reminding her that she wasn't alone. But as the sun rose and set to that first day, she felt more alone than ever.

The dawn of the second day came earlier than anyone in the group felt prepared for. As silently as the day before, they packed up camp and mounted their horses. The wind in the air had a distinctly fall flavor to it, and Sophia shivered a little as they rode. Leaves of every color surrounded her as they continued through the forest, it was almost like a miraculous change had happened overnight. *Although it's not like I've been paying close attention to the weather with everything else going on.* She sighed, trying to release some of the pressure building inside her. She heard a horse pulling up beside her and turned to see…

"Duncan?" surprise clear in her voice.

"Mind if I ride with you for a stretch?"

"Of course not. But wouldn't you prefer to ride with Helen?"

"Seems we'll have plenty of time for that later," he said with a small smile. "Besides, I had some questions I wanted to ask you."

"Questions?"

"About God," he replied.

"Oh," Sophia said uncertainly. She had been surprised by Duncan's assertion that going to Suffrom with Helen was God's plan. He'd never particularly seemed interested in the One True God before, although he hadn't been as vocally opposed as Phillip was. "What did you want to ask?"

"Why do you believe in Him?"

The question took her aback. She'd grown up surrounded by her parents' faith and naturally had accepted it as her own. It was only really since she and Helen had gone on this ill-advised adventure of theirs that she had started to question her own faith. "I...I guess I never really thought about it before."

"Surely you've questioned the existence of God?"

"I have. But I guess He's always just felt real to me."

"Felt real. What do you mean by that?"

She shrugged. "I've heard Him speak to me, I guess." She paused, remembering the voice that spoke to her during her kidnapping. "He reminds me that I'm not alone, that He is always with me."

Duncan nodded, a contemplative look on his face. "The gods I've always heard about never speak to their followers."

"And, I guess my faith in Him gives me hope."

"Hope?"

"Hope that things are going to be okay, even when it doesn't feel like it." She let her gaze drop to the ground in front of her. Leaves crunched under the horses' feet with every step. "Find rest, O my soul, in God alone; my hope comes from him," she muttered quietly to herself. The new words on her mother's sword came flooding back to her, affirming her words and bringing a slight smile to her face.

"What was that?"

"Nothing," she said, turning back to face Duncan. "Did you have any other questions?"

"Not at this time, milady," he said with a slight bow of his head. "I believe the rest of my questions must be addressed to God Himself, if He does exist."

They continued to ride in silence for a few moments before Sophia asked, "Do you love her?"

"Pardon?" Duncan said with a start. "Love whom?"

"Helen. Do you love her? Is that why you're going to Suffrom with her?"

Uncertain of how to respond, Duncan coughed and cleared his throat. Finally, he softly replied, "Perhaps I'm beginning to. She is nothing like anyone I've ever met. I," he stopped to look Sophia in the eyes. "I don't know that I could go back to life without her."

"That's how I feel about God."

Duncan's eyes widened. Sophia continued. "I know that Helen doesn't believe, so I've seen what that looks like. And sometimes, it looks better, less complicated I suppose, than believing in him. But when I really look at my life, I don't know what it would be like without my faith."

Duncan nodded solemnly. "Thank you for answering my questions, milady."

"Why so formal all of a sudden? You've never been that way before."

He shrugged. "It felt right. You may not look it, but Phillip and I both know who you and Helen really are."

A prick of unidentifiable emotion pierced her heart at the mention of Phillip. That was going to be another question that would have to be answered soon.

When the group stopped to camp for the night, they dispersed to their respective corners. Helen approached Duncan, who was starting the process of lighting a fire for the night. He glanced up at her quickly before returning back to his work.

"What were you talking with Sophia about before?"

"God," he said matter of factly.

"Seriously?" she said with disgust.

"I meant what I said, that I think it's possible God brought us together."

"God didn't have anything to do with it. It was just luck."

"Luck brought you into that clearing at the exact moment that we were passing through?"

"Sure," she said, flipping her loose hair back over her shoulder.

"And I suppose luck brought us to the village of your childhood friend, and a man apparently out for revenge on your family?"

"What else?"

"And luck is the reason I'm falling in love with you?"

Helen choked and then stuttered her reply, "What are you talking about?"

Duncan stood to his feet, brushing the dirt from his hands as the fire flickered to life. The seriousness of his expression gave her shivers as he looked her in the eye. "You didn't know?"

"Well," she swallowed nervously, "I just thought you were being chivalrous. You know, since you and Phillip seem to do the hero thing for a living."

"No," he said, continuing to analyze her every move. Nervously, she took a step back from him and started to turn away.

"I should probably check on Sophia…" His hand reached out and grabbed her wrist. She angrily pulled away and shoved him back with both hands. "What's wrong with you?"

"It's time to stop running, Helen."

"I'm not running; I said that I needed to check on…"

"You've been running since the moment I met you. That's what put you and Sophia on this path to begin with." His statement startled her into silence. She stared at him slack-jawed as he continued. "You said you blamed God for your father's death, so you've been running from Him. You've been running from the mother you claim holds no love for you. And because you claim you don't deserve love, you're willing to run at the first sight of it." Duncan stepped forward and took her hand in both of his. "But I believe that this was God's plan all along. You couldn't run away from Him because running from Him brought you to me. You are what makes me want to believe in God."

"But I don't…"

"I know. You don't believe. Perhaps I will have to believe enough for the both of us right now." Gentle as a flower petal, he touched his lips to the back of her hand.

A cheer erupted from across the camp. Both turned to see Phillip beaming from ear to ear, applauding and cheering. "It's about time!" he called, laughter licking at the edge of his voice.

Helen pulled her hand free from Duncan's grasp and turned her bright red face away from him, storming off into the forest muttering something about more firewood. Duncan remained standing by the fire, a slight smirk on his face as he watched her fade into the distance.

"Oh dear," Sophia sighed. She stroked the mane of her horse absentmindedly as she watched her cousin storm off into the forest. A quick glance in Phillip's direction confirmed that he was still laughing quietly to himself. It was good to hear him laugh again. She chuckled quietly. *It feels good to laugh again. Perhaps there can be joy in reality after all?*

"Glad to see I'm not the only one that takes pleasure in other people's discomfort." Phillip flashed a smile to accompany his statement.

"It's good for her, she deserves to have someone love her like that." Sophia sighed. "She'll come around eventually. Especially if he plans on accompanying her to Suffrom."

Phillip's smile darkened at the mention of his friend's soon departure. "Yeah, I guess they'll have plenty of time to figure it out." He finished adjusting the straps he was working with and turned to pick up the food satchel, slinging the strap over his shoulder as he started to walk away.

Chapter Sixteen

The morning of the third day dawned with a chill in the air. A light wind blew through the forest, making Sophia shiver as she saddled her horse. Her soft sigh was slightly visible as a mist puffing out of her mouth. *Winter is coming faster than we could have anticipated.* A quick glance revealed everyone else almost ready to leave, but it was Jacob that caught her attention. Clearly, he was the most unprepared for a shift in the weather like this, and she frowned as he blew into his hands to warm them up. His visible breath chilled her more than the wind.

"Here. Take this."

Jacob looked up with surprise at the blanket Sophia held out to him. Taking it from her quickly, he hung his head. "Thank you. I know I don't deserve it."

"Of course you do." She tilted her head to one side, confused. "Your father is the one who is to blame for all of this, not you."

"But," he spoke so softly she could barely hear his reply, "I helped him. I could have stopped him…"

She waved his answer away; shaking her head slightly. "We all make mistakes. Regardless, I would be making a mistake if I denied you warmth as punishment."

"Can you ever forgive me?"

"I already have," she said before turning away to finish packing her bags.

The group once again rode in silence for most of the day, each one lost in his or her own thoughts. Sophia was feeling more like her old self after her brief conversation with Jacob this morning, so she decided to seek out Phillip to continue cheering her up. When she pulled her horse up alongside his, he barely noticed her.

"A lot on your mind today?"

"I suppose," he muttered.

"About Duncan?"

He refused to make eye contact. "Why would I be thinking about him. I'm happy for him...and your cousin too. He deserves someone who makes him happy."

Sophia laughed lightly, "I don't know if she'll make him happy or keep him guessing! But yes, they deserve each other. What about you?"

He felt a slight burn blossoming on his cheeks. "What about me?"

"What will you do, you know, after we send them on their way and return Jacob to his village?" She waited expectantly for an answer; but when none came, she pressed on. "Will you continue your travels?"

"I suppose."

"Where will you go?"

"What's with all the sudden concern for my plans, Sophia? What does it matter to you?"

She blushed. "I suppose it doesn't; I was just making conversation. You don't have to answer if you don't want to."

Embarrassed by his outburst, Phillip groaned. "I apologize, that was unnecessary." He cleared his throat and glanced her way. She was looking down at the reins in her hand, withdrawing further inward with every passing moment. "What will you do?" She met his gaze with wide-eyed surprise. "When this is all over? Will you return home?"

"Of course. That was always my plan. I had hoped Helen would return with me, but it appears that wasn't meant to be." She grimaced. "I'm going to have to face both of our parents myself. I know Mother and Father will be understanding, but Aunt Ralyn...there's no telling how she'll react."

"I'm sure you'll be able to explain everything to their satisfaction."

She smiled. "What makes you so sure?"

"Because," he said, trying to keep his grin to a minimum, "you always do."

Another blush spread across her face. "Thank you for your confidence, I suppose."

"Hey, if you can make Duncan a believer in the One True God, you must be a magician with words." He laughed but stopped suddenly when he realized he was alone. Sophia was looking at him with such urgency it gave him pause. "Sophia?"

"What about you?"

"What about me?"

"Could I ever explain the One True God to you in a way that would make you believe? What could I say that would change your mind?"

"No. There is nothing that will change my mind."

Uncertain how to reply, she said nothing. She said nothing as Phillip pulled away from her and left her riding alone. And she said nothing as the tears started to flow in little rivulets down her face. *Why does this feel so important to me? Why do I care what he believes?* With more questions than answers, she brushed her tears away and focused on the journey that still lay in front of her.

It was late in the day when the group saw what looked like ruins in the near distance. Outlined against the sky were large stone structures of varying heights, most appeared to be in disrepair.

"I don't remember there being a settlement or village this close to the border; do you, Sophia?"

A silent shake of her head was the only reply Helen got. With a roll of her eyes, she turned her attention back to the ruins. *Whatever that idiot Phillip said to her has her really upset...I'm going to have to have a talk with him later.* For the moment, she tried to wrack her brain for anything on the maps they studied growing up that would tell her what these ruins were. "Perhaps we've moved too far west in our travels?"

"I don't think so," Duncan said, coming up behind her. The five of them had stopped to water the horses at a fairly large stream they'd stumbled upon. Duncan was the one who'd pointed out the ruins, lying directly in their path. They would reach them before the end of the day. Sophia still stood silently staring alternately at the ground and the horizon. Conveniently, Phillip had volunteered to take care of the horses, and Jacob was helping him. With her own emotions being so confused right now, Helen felt incapable of dealing with Sophia's problems as well. *Almost home. If I can just get back to Suffrom, then everything will be alright. I'll be free to be who I want, and I can finally be the Queen I was born to be. What will Mother say then?* A sharp pain shot through her heart at the reminder of her mother. *I don't want to deal with that right now either.*

"Duncan," she said, turning her attention elsewhere as a distraction, "where do you think we are?"

"I'm uncertain; but I do know that we have been traveling due south since the return of Sophia to our party. However, it is possible that prior to our arrival in the village we were traveling more southwest than we intended. If that is so then…"

"You'll need to cross the Senden River that runs along the southwestern border of Adven," Sophia said, finally engaging in the conversation. She glanced up to meet Helen's gaze. "If that's the case, then I know where we are."

Her shoes made soft clicking noises as she walked across the stone floor of what appeared at one time to be a dining hall. Two of the walls had completely collapsed, leaving only two partially constructed stone walls standing on the east and north of the room. In the wreckage, Sophia could picture what the room had once looked like, filled with laughter and people. She sat on a pile of forgotten building materials, trying to take the scene in.

The summer palace was a rumor that had practically faded from existence in recent history. According to her mother's stories when she was younger, the palace had fallen during a battle in the war during the childhood of her mother, Queen Aimi. Although it had always been his intention to repair it, King Andrew was never able to fulfill the promise he made to his queen before she died. After her death, Katherine said her father had never been the same. He became angry and impulsive, which ultimately led to his obsession with destroying Jacob's father and the army he'd raised.

But the queen spoke of how she and Aunt Ralyn had planned on repairing the summer palace and returning it to its former glory. When they were girls they talked about picnics by the riverside and days spent picking flowers in the gardens. *It would have been beautiful. I'm sorry they never got to see their dream come to fruition.* Sophia shook her head. It was odd to think of her mother and Aunt Ralyn as girls, dreaming about rebuilding a castle for them to play in.

"Sophia?"

Phillip poked his head around one of the remaining walls. He had a concerned look on his face, which made her smile. "Helen asked me to speak with you."

A stifled laugh. "Did she?"

He ran a nervous hand through his hair as he walked toward her. "Well I suppose *ask* is a generous interpretation of our conversation." He sighed as he sat down on the stone beside her. "I wanted to apologize earlier for my thoughtless behavior. It was unkind of me and completely unnecessary."

"Apology accepted. I wasn't really mad; I just worry about you."

An awkward silence followed. Finally speaking to break the silence, "I appreciate it."

"Appreciate what?" Sophia asked, puzzled.

"Your worry. Duncan is the only one who's ever worried about me before and he..." A pause. "Well, he'll be gone soon."

"You've never really told me how the two of you met."

"We were orphans. Both of our parents died when we were young; and an old woman took us in, along with any other orphans in the surrounding villages. After that, we were always together." A sad smile. "But I guess it's time for us to part ways. I should have known we couldn't stay together forever."

"Helen and I have always been together as well," Sophia said softly. "It will be difficult to return home without her." An uncomfortable pause, followed by a quiet cough. "I wanted to ask if you'd return home with me?"

A single raised eyebrow was his response. "Return home?"

She nodded. "I wouldn't really feel comfortable traveling all that way by myself. I'd always planned on convincing Helen to return with me, remember?"

"Oh," he replied, swallowing hard to buy time. Then he smiled. "I would be honored to accompany you, milady." Phillip jumped up from his seat and offered an awkward bow.

She laughed, covering her hand with her mouth to try and control it. "I accept your service, my good knight."

It was their laughter that filled the ruins as the sun set, filling the sky with its bright oranges and pinks over the cold gray of the stones around them.

Chapter Seventeen

Without the trees to block the wind, it blew in stronger gusts than she expected. Sophia breathed the fresh air with a deep breath and released it with a smile. The Senden River was the wildest body of water she had ever seen, with waves whipping against the rocks at the bottom of the cliffs in front of her. Many years ago, crossing would have been a quick process of riding a boat from one side to the other. However, now the river had dug a deep chasm, almost a mile deep; creating a distinctive gap that served as the border between Adven and Suffrom. Had they ridden directly south, as was their original intention from the castle, they would have avoided the river and instead crossed easily over the plains that lay in the southeastern part of the country.

But she didn't mind. While Helen fumed about the delay this would cause, she had determined to enjoy the home of her mother's dreams. *It is incredibly restful. I can understand why Mother wanted to rebuild it.*

Jacob had spent a restless night trying to understand Sophia's words to him the morning before. *How can she forgive me?* He was determined to confront her about it today. He had no idea how long they would be stopping here before Helen and Duncan would cross the border to Suffrom while Sophia and Phillip returned with him to his village. *I have to know…if she can forgive me, then perhaps my family…*

He'd found her standing on the edge of the cliff overlooking the river. And quite a picture it was! The wind was blowing the loose strands of hair from her face, fluttering like stray ribbons. Her dress swayed around her ankles, heavy enough to not blow too much but light enough to still be lifted in the breeze. At her side hung her ever present sword, reminding him of the princess she was. She wasn't looking at him as he approached, completely lost in the scenery around her.

"Your Majesty?"

Startled, she spun around, breaking the picturesque moment. "Another thing I've ruined," he muttered to himself. "Pardon my interruption, but I wondered if I may speak with you?"

"Of course, Jacob. What is it?"

He paused, flustered for a moment. "I wanted to continue our conversation from yesterday…"

"There was nothing to continue," Sophia interrupted. "I do not blame you for all of the actions of your father, and I forgive you for the actions that were your own. What more did you want me to say?"

"It is not what I wished *you* to say, but what I wished to say to you."

She waited for more, crossing her arms against the chill in the air.

Jacob paused again, struggling to find the right words for what he wanted to say. "I cannot accept your forgiveness, milady."

"And why not?"

"Because I don't deserve it."

"Everyone deserves forgiveness. It is lack of forgiveness that causes problems like the revenge your father craves."

"Then I cannot accept it because I do not want it."

She paused, waiting for further explanation.

"If I cannot forgive myself, how can I ask for your forgiveness?" He closed his eyes, feeling tears forming against his will.

A gentle hand on his shoulder startled him, causing him to fling his eyes open and releasing the tears that had been hiding. Sophia's soft brown eyes met his with tears of her own. "If God forgives you and I forgive you, then why can you not forgive yourself?"

"Because I abandoned him!" Jacob said with fierceness. "I knew what He expected of me, the rules I should have followed, and I chose to follow my father instead!" He hung his head in shame, letting the tears fall as they may. "How can the One True God ever forgive me for this?"

"Because that is who He is," Sophia said softly. "I know it doesn't make sense, but…that is who He is."

"Fools, both of you."

The two of them turned around to see a bedraggled old man approaching, carrying a sword in one hand and bearing a sadistic grin.

"Father!" Jacob stood protectively in front of Sophia, throwing an arm out to stop her from approaching the intruder. "I did not expect you to catch up with us so quickly."

"You think so little of me, my foolish boy. I will not give up on my revenge so easily." He brandished the sword menacingly. "Now move aside. I have business with this girl."

"Jacob," Sophia said, gently pushing him out of the way. "This is between your father and I." She drew her sword and held it loosely beside her. "It is time we settle this feud. May I make a request?"

The old man sneered at her without replying.

"If you kill me, will you leave the rest of my family alone?"

"I suppose I could consider my revenge complete. Is that all?"

"And you will leave Jacob and his family alone as well?"

"Your Majesty," Jacob said in protest. "You don't have to do that."

"Be silent, you worthless fool," his father said. He smiled as he readied himself to fight. "As you wish. I never considered him a son worth my time anyway."

Sophia nodded in assent and placed her sword in front of her.

Immediately, he was upon her, bringing his sword down on her head in a crushing blow. She threw her sword up to block, using all her strength to fling him backward. He responded immediately, bringing his sword out to strike her midsection; which she blocked with difficulty, holding her sword across her like a shield.

He's surprisingly strong for an old man. But I guess I shouldn't be surprised he's strong enough to fight like this. Sophia tried to attack him by swinging at his unprotected left side, but he flicked her sword away like she was a child. Anger broiled inside her as she attacked. Again, she swung at his side, this time aiming for the right; but he blocked her again, this time almost knocking the sword from her grasp. She drew back, breathing hard as she tried to reevaluate her approach.

But he did not draw back, instead bringing his sword down on her head once more. *I can't block it in time. I left myself over extended with my last attack. God...*

Her prayer was cut off and replaced by a scream that ripped from her throat like it was being pulled from her very soul. She hastily tried to pull her sword up to block, knowing it was a futile effort. But then, she felt herself being pushed backward as someone jumped in front of her. The sword meant for her cut deep through the chest of the man, falling back against her as he fell. Her own sword fell to the ground as she caught her savior.

"Jacob?" she gasped. His shirt was covered with blood, more and more with each second that passed. Rattling breaths came in short gasps as he struggled to keep breathing. The old man shook his head in disgust as he cleaned his sword in the grass. Ripping part of her underdress with strength she didn't know she possessed, Sophia pressed the scrap of cloth into the wound and tried to stop the bleeding. "Jacob? Please don't...please don't die. I didn't mean for..."

"It's alright," he wheezed. His eyes rolled towards her lazily. "Does he...does he really forgive me?"

"Yes," she said, tears appearing at the corners of her eyes. "Of course, God forgives you. That's...that's who he is."

"Thank you." His chest stopped shuddering, and his eyes lost their focus, staring emptily at the sky. Sophia released the bloodstained cloth and sat back in shock.

"Fool."

She glanced up at her opponent, forgotten for the moment. "You killed him. Your own son."

"That idiot was no son of mine."

"That's all you have to say?"

He shrugged. "I've no words to waste on him."

Gently, Sophia moved Jacob's head from her lap to the ground. She stood on shaking feet, picking up her sword as she did so. "No more words? Your son was a better man than you will ever be!" she screamed as she leaped over the body, swinging her sword at the man's head as she did so.

Suddenly, she felt the hilt grow hot as it had on that night so long ago, but this time it did not burn. Instead it felt like the warmth of holding her father's hand when she was a little girl. A bright light illuminated the arc of the sword, as well as the sword itself, as it came crashing toward her enemy. Surprised, he managed to throw up his sword as a block at the last minute, but her strength seemed to have tripled. Like lightening she withdrew to strike again and again, each time pushing him back further and further.

Unbeknownst to both of them, the cliff's edge suddenly drew dangerously close, as his backward step landed on a crumbling piece of earth. Startled, he dropped his sword, letting it clang repeatedly against the sides of the cliff as it tumbled into the river. His hand reached out and grabbed at Sophia's dress, trying to stabilize himself. She slapped his hand away with her free hand, dropping her sword and letting it land on the grass beside her. Then she pushed with both hands as the old man tried to wrap his wrinkled fingers around her wrist. Angrily, she broke free of his grip and stepped back, only to watch him lose his balance completely and tumble over the side of the cliff, an unearthly scream accompanying his fall. In horror, she fell backwards onto the grass beside her fallen sword, trying desperately to catch her breath.

It's over. I...I killed him. She glanced at Jacob's pale form stretched out behind her. *And he killed Jacob.*

"Sophia!"

She turned to see Helen, Duncan, and Phillip coming around the ruins to her left. Unable to move, she allowed them to come to her. Helen immediately dropped to her knees and pulled Sophia into her arms. "We heard screaming and came running, but we were all the way on the other side of the ruins. What happened? Who did this to you? Sophia, you're covered in blood!"

"It's not mine...I don't think." She was feeling a little dizzy, maybe she was injured? "Jacob he..." She dissolved into tears, gut-wrenching sobs wracking her body. With each sob, her side throbbed. Instinctively, she pressed her hands against the unseen wound, gasping with the sudden influx of sharp pain. "Helen, I..." She pulled away from her cousin's embrace and looked at her hands, covered in blood. How could she tell if it was hers or...her gaze traveled over to where Jacob lay on the grass, alone. "Please..." She let out another cry of pain before slumping over against Helen, passing into the bliss of unconsciousness.

Chapter Eighteen

"We have to go back to the village, Helen, they're the best hope for Sophia. Her wound means she cannot ride as far or fast each day; so it'll take a little longer, but they have more medical knowledge than I do."

Duncan's voice was calm and even as he explained the situation. Helen was still frantically pacing, disturbing the fallen leaves around her as she walked. A fire crackled softly in between them, keeping the unconscious Sophia warm as she slept. After giving them a brief explanation of what had occurred, she'd passed out from exhaustion. Currently, she lay stretched out on the grass and covered with blankets next to Duncan, who had cleaned and bandaged the cut in her side. He insisted it was nothing too serious, but that she may be in need of medicine if it were to get infected. Phillip had disappeared off to who knows where.

"But I can't just leave." Helen stopped her pacing to look at the other side of the chasm. "Suffrom is right there," she cried, gesturing to punctuate her point. "I can't just go back when I'm so close."

"Sophia needs to go back, immediately."

"Then Phillip can take her back."

"I won't send him alone with an injured woman; even if it is just a few days journey."

"Then go with him! I'll go to Suffrom myself."

"No," Duncan replied firmly.

The anger and worry boiling inside her spilled over as she marched over to where he was seated on the ground. "You don't get to make decisions for me. I get to make my own choices. How dare you try to tell me what to do! Do whatever you want, but don't you dare try to stop me!"

"Helen," he said, standing to meet her gaze face to face. "We decided that I was going with you, and that has not changed. I promise," he took her hand as he spoke, wrapping her quivering fingers with both of his hands, "I will take you to Suffrom. But for now, we must take care of Sophia. Do you wish your cousin to die simply from lack of care of a treatable wound?"

"Of course not," she stuttered, distracted by the warmth of his hands. "I just…" She looked up at him, for once at a loss for words. "I can't go back," she finally whispered breaking eye contact as she pulled away and crossed her arms. "You don't understand…my mother, she…that castle, it…" Tears were threatening to appear, but she squeezed her eyes shut angrily. "I was dying there, lost in that world. I was so alone. My mother might as well have died with my father; she just gave up living. And I was trapped in a world I could never be a part of. Sophia and Solomon, Uncle Michael and Aunt Katherine…they couldn't replace what I lost…what I never had."

She turned once again toward the other side of the chasm, seemingly beckoning her to jump across with a leap of faith. Helen sighed in frustration as the tears escaped their capture. "I just wanted to start over. I wanted to build my own life, where maybe I had a chance for a different ending. I couldn't just stay there, reminded every day of what I lost. That's why I had to leave…and why I can't go back."

Duncan silently walked up beside her, stopping to look at the horizon with his hands clasped behind him. "I understand."

Surprised, she turned her tear stained face toward him. "You do?"

"My parents died when I was a child. There was a fire; my father carried me to safety at my mother's insistence and then returned to rescue her. But he wasn't fast enough." He closed his eyes, remembering. "So, I was taken in by an elderly woman in our village. She had a full house of orphaned children, including myself and not too long after that Phillip came to join us. He…well let's say he was determined to be friends." A smile at the memory.

"As we grew up, we watched many of the other children gain apprenticeships, get married, have children of their own. However, I always knew that I could never stay in that village once I came of age. The memory of my parents' death was…" he paused, looking for the right words. "Too painful."

"So that was why you and Phillip left and became traveling swordsmen."

He smiled again. "There's a bit more to it than that, but yes, in short we both felt a new life would benefit both of us."

Helen spoke earnestly, "Then you understand why I can't go back?"

"I understand why you think you can't go back."

"But you just said…"

He spoke softly, barely above a whisper as he met her gaze. "I understand the desire to start over. But I realize now that I never needed to leave the village to find my new start. The answer was right in front of me, in the stories I heard from the elderly woman who raised me, but I didn't understand. She spoke of a God who would be my father, even though I had lost my own. I did not realize until hearing Sophia speak about her belief in the One True God that they were speaking of the same person.

So many in our land believe the gods are dead. They do not hear our prayers. They do not give second chances. But, Helen, the One True God has given me the greatest gift I could ever ask for…He gave me you, if you will have me."

Helen took a step backward, struggling for a response as she blushed bright red. "I don't understand."

"I told you that I believed God brought us together. I told you that I am falling in love with you. What more is there to understand?" His smile faded. "Do you not feel the same way about me?"

Her blush spread further across her face and touched the tips of her ears. "I wouldn't say that exactly…"

"Well then? What else is there to understand?"

"How can you believe that easily?"

"Because it makes the most sense. Do you not agree?"

"I'm not sure yet." Helen held out her hand, and he took it. "But I'd like to find out."

Duncan pulled her close; and she let him, allowing herself to be enveloped in his embrace. He kissed her lightly on the top of her head, and she felt the warmth of his love spread down to her toes. *This is what I've always wanted. To feel loved like this.*

"Pardon the interruption…"

The couple pulled apart, startled by the sudden intrusion. Sophia sat, propped up on one elbow, grinning from ear to ear.

"Sophia, you're awake!" Helen rushed to her side and helped her sit up the rest of the way. "How are you feeling?"

"Like I was in a sword fight," she said with a slight chuckle. "Where's Phillip?"

The shovel chipped away at the ground, slowly building a deeper and deeper ditch below his feet. With each mound of dirt he tossed away, he groaned from the effort. *When was the last time I dug a hole?* Phillip brushed the sweat away from his brow with a sweep of his hand. Even with the colder autumn temperatures, he was sweating up a storm. *Then again, this isn't just a hole…it's a grave.*

Although he didn't approve of the man's actions over the past few days, he couldn't stand the idea of denying him a proper burial. So, Phillip had taken it upon himself to dig a grave on the cliffside where they had found Jacob and Sophia. *I hope she's alright.* It was a convenient coincidence that it provided an alternative to keep his mind busy, other than worrying about Sophia.

With the grave finally finished, he carefully lowered the body wrapped in blankets. "I suppose I should say something," he muttered to himself. He leaned against the shovel handle, digging a slight dent into the soil beneath him.

"Jacob, I…" he cleared his throat. "I don't really know what to say right now. I didn't know you that well and when I did know you, I didn't trust you." *Oh, great. This is turning out to be an excellent eulogy, Phillip.*

He sat down on the dying grass, letting the shovel remain standing up stuck partway in the ground. "What I mean to say is that, I really do appreciate what you did for Sophia, how you rescued her from your father even though it meant revealing what you had done to us. I know you didn't mean for any harm to come to her. I guess I could have been a little more understanding of your situation, couldn't I?" He ran his hand through his hair, realized how muddy his hands were, then proceeded to brush the dirt off absentmindedly. "Jacob, what I'm trying to say is that I forgive you, okay? I know that really doesn't mean anything now that you're..." Another awkward pause. "Well, you know. But I do forgive you for what you did. I'm sorry I didn't realize it sooner."

He brushed the dirt from his pants, or made a halfhearted attempt at it anyway, and pulled the shovel from the ground. Then slowly he began to fill in the grave, each pile of dirt burying a heavier burden within his heart.

"Phillip?"

He turned around, just as he finished putting the last shovelful of dirt on the grave. "Sophia?" Tossing aside his shovel, he rushed to her, starting to pull her into a hug before thinking better of it. "How are you? Should you be up and around like that?"

She shrugged, pulling at the blanket wrapped around her shoulders. Moving slightly to her right, she peered around Phillip to see the grave beyond.

"Is that...?"

He nodded. "Yes, I felt it best to bury him as quickly as possible. I didn't know how soon we would be leaving again."

"Duncan seems to think we should return to the village immediately," she grimaced in pain, reaching instinctively to touch her side. "He's worried about infection or something."

"He's right to be worried," Phillip said with concern as he followed her hand movement with his eyes.

She sidestepped around him and walked toward the grave. "He saved me."

"I know, you've told us."

"No," she interrupted. "That's how he died. His father followed us here and attacked me. I tried to fight him off, but I," she

162

shook her head, trying to shake away the memory. "I let him trick me into overextending myself. But Jacob jumped in front of the blow. He died saving me." She hung her head in shame, letting the tears flow freely.

Phillip put his hand on her shoulder, gently turning her around to face him. "Then he died a hero."

"He died asking me if God forgave him for what he did," she snapped. "I told him I forgave him, that God forgave him…why wouldn't he believe me?"

"Maybe he felt like he had to earn it."

"But he didn't," she insisted. "I didn't want anything from him. Why did he feel like he had to save me?" She was struggling to continue speaking as she choked on her angry tears. "Phillip, he died in my arms. And there was nothing I could do about it."

Uncertain how to respond, he pulled her closer to him. Sophia buried her face in his chest, letting out gasping sobs. "Why, Phillip? Why didn't God stop this from happening?"

Hesitant to comment, he decided to change the topic. "What happened after that, Sophia? What happened to Jacob's father?"

The sobs immediately stopped, and her whole body stiffened. "I killed him."

"What?"

"I killed him!" she cried, pulling away from Phillip, eyes wild and dropping the blanket as she stepped backward. "I don't know what came over me, but my sword…" She glanced down at her right hand as though she held the sword still. "There was a light, and then I was fighting him. It felt like someone else was fighting with me. And suddenly, we were on the edge of the cliff, and he…" She trailed off, lost in thought.

Phillip approached slowly, picking up the fallen blanket and rewrapping it around her shoulders. "I think we should find Helen and Duncan and call it a night. I'm sure he'll want to head out in the morning."

She silently nodded and let herself be led away from the grave.

Early the next morning, the group packed up their belongings and headed out for the village. Sophia was quiet, reflective, and slightly pensive. She had refused to carry her sword, instead strapping it to Phillip's horse with their supplies. While she couldn't deny that the death of Jacob's father was good for her and her family, she hated the part she'd had to play in it.

I've never killed anyone before. Adam had trained her and Helen since they were children in the art of swordsmanship; but with the kingdom at peace it seemed impossible she would ever have to fight like her mother had.

I miss Mother. The admission, even silently to herself, was enough to bring tears to her eyes. She wished that they were headed back to the palace instead of the village. In the village Jacob's wife and newborn son would be waiting for him to return.

Which he never will...because of me. Shaking her head to rid herself of her worries for the moment, she gently nudged her horse to move faster. "The sooner we get there; the sooner we can get home," she whispered under her breath.

Chapter Nineteen

At first, the door wouldn't budge. He had to press his shoulder against the wood to get it open. Although nothing blocked the door, the hinges were beginning to stick from lack of use. Nothing had changed, not a single piece of clothing or speck of dust. Everything was exactly as it had been the last time he was commanded to leave this room. Since then, no one had been allowed entrance.

But I mustn't give up. I promised Her Majesty. Eli tried to ignore the little puffs of dust that rose as he walked through the room. A few footsteps were apparent here and there, but nothing of significance. The balcony door was open, allowing the crisp fall air to lift the edges of the curtains slightly. Ralyn remained in her chair, staring at the dying garden without feeling. She didn't acknowledge Eli as he stepped onto the balcony and gently put his hand on her shoulder.

"Ralyn, can you hear me?"

She nodded. There was no use continuing to ignore him.

"You must eat, child."

"My childhood was dashed to dust years ago."

"You will always be a child to me, Ralyn. You and Katherine were like my own daughters." He shifted his tone to a sterner variation. "And it is my responsibility to take care of you, especially when you won't do it yourself."

A cough escaped her lips, and she pressed her hand against her mouth, coughing into it with difficulty. When it subsided, she replied, "I commanded you to leave me alone. That forgives you your responsibility."

"It is not that easily forgiven."

She closed her eyes and breathed heavily. There was a slight rattle to her breathing if he listened closely. Eli's next words were even more insistent. "You must eat, Ralyn. You're ill; you need your strength."

"No."

Her flat refusal surprised him. "No? You will die if you don't eat. You can't keep on like this!" He felt himself shaking, shivering with cold and fear at the implications of her words.

"So be it."

Eli tried to meet her gaze, but her eyes remained closed. She was shutting him out, as she had shut out the rest of the world. "Child, don't do this. Your life does not have to be over. You have people who love you. Helen will come back, and spring will come again," he said with a gesture to the garden of dead flowers and weeds below them. Then after a pause, "God still loves you, Ralyn. You are not too far gone."

"Don't speak to me of God, old man," she sneered. Her voice raised with each word as she continued. "He has done nothing but bring me misery and pain. My faith in him was foolish; perhaps he never existed at all, or perhaps he has just forgotten me. God will not save me now." She dissolved into coughing, this time using a handkerchief to cover her mouth for the next few minutes. Eli noticed specks of blood as she set it back in her lap when the fit subsided. "Leave now, and this time don't return."

His heart weary and his spirit broken, Eli slowly walked back out of the room, closing the door behind him with a quiet sigh.

Five days felt like an eternity as they passed through the forest once again. Sophia was lost in her own thoughts and memories, completely oblivious to her surroundings. The memory of Jacob's death and the events that followed replayed in her mind over and over like a dream. At night her sleep was constantly interrupted as she awoke almost every hour screaming. Phillip and Helen tried to comfort her, but inevitably she ended up sitting by the fire for hours in silence. The guilt was tearing her apart.

She barely noticed as the trees thinned and they passed into the clearing hosting the village. She didn't say a word as they were greeted by villagers, who happily took their horses and sent a messenger ahead to warn Lilly of their arrival. She moved as a ghost, floating through the town as they made their way to the familiar cottage.

It wasn't until they opened the door to see a familiar face seated at Lilly's table that she finally released the dam of sorrow barely locked away in her heart.

"Mother," she sobbed, collapsing into Queen Katherine's arms as her friends and family looked on.

"Here, take this." A bowl and spoon were pressed into her empty hands, and she took them without argument. The broth tasted warm against her throat as she ate it a spoonful at a time.

"When you were a little girl you loved slurping that up in one big gulp, much to my dismay." Katherine gently tucked Sophia's hair behind her ear as she spoke. When Michael, Solomon, and the rest of their entourage had arrived at the village, she had been surprised to hear Lilly's account of her daughter and niece's arrival and sudden departure. Certain that they would eventually return, Michael had convinced her, against her will, to remain there while they waited for news. As happy as she was to have her little girl back with her, it was clear there were some unresolved issues that needed to be discussed.

"Sophia, your companions have told me a little of what happened since you were last here; but I would like to hear it from you."

She set down her bowl and spoon, half finished. "There was a man. He was following us; I don't know for how long. Apparently, he was an old enemy of yours?" She paused and looked for confirmation. Katherine silently nodded, not wanting to add to the story at the moment. Sophia looked back down at her lap as she continued speaking. "He kidnapped me and dragged me into the forest. I thought he was going to kill me, but a man we'd met here in the village rescued me."

"Jacob?"

"Yes," her voice dropped to a whisper, "it turns out the man who'd kidnapped me was actually his father. They were working

167

together, but then Jacob decided to betray him and save me instead. He came with us to the border." She shifted and met her mother's gaze for a moment. "We found the summer castle, Mother, the one you and Aunt Ralyn used to talk about. It was abandoned and destroyed, but I remembered it from your stories. The plan was for Helen and Duncan to cross the border together, while Phillip and I returned back home."

"And Jacob?"

"We were going to pass through this village again to bring him home. The plan was to let them decide what was to be done. He was truly ashamed of what his father had convinced him to do." Sophia paused again, seeming to struggle for words. She pulled her knees up to her chest and wrapped her arms around them. "But then his father showed up and attacked me. I tried to defend myself, but he got the better of me. Then Jacob…" she stuttered and struggled to continue. "Jacob…he jumped in front of me. His father…" Her voice cracked, and tears appeared in her eyes. "Then I…" She buried her face in her knees, unable to continue. Muffled sobs could be heard as Katherine gently rubbed her daughter's back.

"I'm sorry, Sophia. This was not what I wanted for you. Your father and I would have done anything to spare you this pain."

Sophia shook her head. "It wasn't your fault. I chose this. Helen and I did when we ran away." The tears continued trickling down her face. "But I didn't…I never imagined…" She threw herself into her mother's embrace. "Why does it hurt so much?"

Tears of her own were threatening to spill over as the queen held her sobbing little girl. "Because life is precious. You understand the sadness that comes from the ending of a life, even a bad one."

"I felt so angry. He had just killed Jacob, his own son; he…he deserved to die," she said hesitantly. "Didn't he, Mother?"

Katherine gathered her thoughts a moment before responding. "God did not make us the judge of mankind." She sighed. "My darling Sophia, I have killed many men in my life. That is unfortunately the nature of war. Did they all deserve it or were there innocents like Jacob who would have chosen otherwise had they been given the chance?" She shook her head. "I will never know the answer until I meet the One True God after my own death...and perhaps he will spare me the pain of knowing even then."

Sophia had stopped shaking and instead stared at her mother, still with her arms wrapped tightly around her knees still pressed to her chest. *She looks so young...God, I wish that it had been me instead of my child.* The Queen rescued the bowl that was tipping precariously over the edge of the bed where her daughter had abandoned it. "Did you know that when I met Edwin he was a soldier in that man's army?"

Eyes opening wide with surprise, Sophia shook her head in an emphatic no.

"Were it not for his help, your father and I would have remained as captives; and God only knows what would have happened then." A faint smile. "It was around that time that I discovered I was pregnant with you, our daughter."

"Really?"

"Indeed," Katherine replied. "Even in a terrible situation, God was still doing good...even though I did not always see it. I gained a husband, a friend, a daughter, and eventually your brother Solomon because of the war that Jacob's father started. Yes, there was loss. My father and your uncle Evan..." she paused, her thoughts drifting to a silent sister seated in a dark room before snapping back to the present. "But, Sophia, even in the darkest situations, God brings light."

Thoughtfully, the young woman nodded. "Mother, do you think good will come out of Jacob's death? Do you think good will come out of...of what I did to his father?" she finished softly.

"I know it will. I do not know what it may be or when it will come; but I believe that God brings good to those who believe in him."

Sophia nodded and remained silent for a few minutes. Hesitantly, she broached the next subject. "What about the sword, Mother?"

"The sword?"

"You said I would know when it was my time to have it. When Helen and I left, she insisted I take it. But when I…when I stole it…there was this light, and it burned my hand." She kept her eyes focused on her mother, trying to read any reaction as she told the story. "After that it changed the words that were etched on it! But there was never a light again until…until after he killed Jacob."

"And what happened then?" her mother said, encouraging her to keep talking.

"There was a light, like before, but it didn't burn me this time. It felt like…like this," she said, taking her mother's hand in her own, "it felt like holding you or Father's hand. And then, I felt so much stronger! It felt like there was someone fighting with me." She ended abruptly and let go of her mother's hand. "That sounds ridiculous now that I say it out loud."

"What do the words say?"

Sophia glanced up, surprised at the question. "Find rest, O my soul, in God alone; my hope comes from him. He alone is my rock and my salvation; he is my fortress, I will not be shaken."

"And what happened right before the light and the warmth?"

"I," she paused, thinking, "I think I was praying. I remember the shock and the anger at seeing Jacob die, but I don't remember much after that."

Katherine smiled. "That sword was a gift from a very special woman, who was very close to the One True God. I believe that God gave the original words to me because they were how I needed to grow in my faith. Perhaps God knew this was where you needed to grow, in where to place your hope and where to build your foundation."

"Do you want it back?"

The Queen shook her head. "I believe the sword has found its next owner. May it protect you as it has protected me over the years."

Sophia nodded, a serious look on her face at the implication that it was God himself who had rescued her. "Thank you, Mother." She smiled and leaned over the side of the bed to give her mother a crushing hug. "I've missed you, so much."

Katherine felt a single tear trying to escape from her eye as she pulled her little girl closer. "I've missed you too."

"So, it sounds like I owe you a debt of gratitude?"

Phillip stood up quickly at the sound of the King's voice. He gave a short bow and kept his eyes averted. *This is Sophia's father. Don't say anything ridiculous, Phillip!* "I can't imagine why, Your Majesty."

"Why? For accompanying my daughter and niece on their journey without anything in return. Is there something I can give you for your service? I feel that nothing can truly express how grateful I am for the safe return of my family."

What I want you can't possibly give me. "Your gratitude is more than enough, Sir. It truly wasn't a problem; we were happy to be of service."

An awkward silence followed as Phillip continued to look at the King's boots. *Nice leather, but they look worn. I wonder if the King has his own personal shoemaker?*

"Phillip, isn't it?"

"Yes, Your Majesty."

"You don't have to be so formal," the King replied with a hint of a smile. "You may call me Michael. I've never quite grown used to all of the titles that come with the crown."

Phillip dared a glance upward and saw the King smiling at him. "Sir?"

With a sigh, Michael sat down beside the fountain, where Phillip had also been sitting just a few minutes before. He stretched out his legs and let his hand dip into the cold water. As the cold of winter approached, fewer and fewer people found themselves socializing in the town square. Most were beginning to prefer the warmth of a hearth within their own homes. However, Lily's home

171

was unable to accommodate all the guests she suddenly found herself hosting. The group had been split up amongst several families, and it had been a couple of days since Phillip had seen Sophia, who was staying at Lily's house. He hadn't spoken to either the King or Queen since the quick introduction on the day of their arrival.

"So why haven't you come to visit my daughter? She's asked about you."

"Sir?"

Michael motioned to the empty space beside him. "Sit down, Phillip. I promise I don't bite often."

"Sir?" Phillip repeated, slight alarm in his voice.

A smile. "It's a joke, son. Just sit down; I feel we should talk."

Edging a few feet away from him, Phillip took a seat beside the fountain...and the King. *Sophia's father. What do I say to him?*

"You haven't answered my question yet."

"What question?"

"Why haven't you come to visit my daughter? She's asked about you."

Because I don't know what to say to her either. "I didn't want to disrupt her healing process, Sir."

Michael waved a hand in the air, dismissing the excuse. "She tougher than that. As I suspect you know. The doctor says she should be ready to travel again in a couple of days." He eyed the young man beside him. "In the meantime, you should visit her. She said you were planning on returning to the castle with her?"

"I was, Sir."

"Call me Michael, please. You make it sound as if you've changed your mind? May I ask why?"

"I suppose she doesn't need my services anymore, Sir...um, Michael, Sir." *Smooth, Phillip.* He cleared his throat to buy a few precious seconds.

"What do you mean?"

"Well, she'll be returning with her family and the rest of your entourage. My, um, protection won't be needed anymore."

"And where will you go then?"

The question caught him by surprise. It shouldn't have, as it had been uppermost in his thoughts over the last few days, first because of Duncan's decision and then the sudden reappearance of Sophia's family. "I don't know, Sir." *Calling the King by his first name just doesn't feel natural.*

"Then why not come with us?"

"Sir?"

Michael laughed. "Are you afraid of me, Phillip?"

"No, Sir." *Maybe a little...*

"Then, I insist on two things. First, drop the 'sir' and call me Michael. And second, return to the castle with us. I understand your friend will be accompanying Helen back to Suffrom; and I would hate to lose the opportunity to avail myself of your services again in the future. Besides," he paused with that smirk returning to his voice, "I believe it would please my daughter greatly were you to fulfill your promise to accompany her home."

A flutter in his chest interrupted any prepared replies to this unexpected gesture. "If you insist...Michael." *That will take some getting used to.*

The King clapped him on the back with a smile before rising and setting off in the direction of Lily's house. Phillip remained in the deserted town square pondering the King's final words. *Will Sophia really be pleased that I'm not leaving just yet?*

"How is she?"

Helen looked up from the book she was lazily flipping through to see Duncan standing before her. "She's getting better, Uncle Michael and Aunt Katherine think they should be able to leave the day after tomorrow."

"And what about you? Have you made a decision?"

"About?" she snipped, irritated at the reminder.

"About our destination."

"We're going to Suffrom, of course. We should travel slightly more eastward, so we can avoid having the cross the river. If we reach the plains by the end of the week then…"

Duncan sat down at the table beside her and took her hand. "Helen, is that really what you want?"

"Of course." She thought about pulling her hand away, but his was so warm…

"Helen," he said softly. "What about your Mother?"

That did make her jerk her hand out of his and slam the book shut in the same quick motion. "What about her?"

"Do you really never want to see her again?"

"Who says I'll never see her again? I'll go back to visit in a year or so. It's not like she'll even notice I'm gone; she barely noticed me when I was there."

"Is that what you really think?"

His voice was so gentle, it made her feel something she'd never felt stir in her chest. *Was this how you felt about Father? Did you ever feel this way about me?* She shook the questions away and met his gaze. "What good would it do anyway? She probably doesn't want to see me again. I remind her of Father."

"Perhaps. Or perhaps she realizes how much she loves you now that you've been gone for so long. Perhaps she wants a second chance."

"She doesn't deserve one."

"Just like you didn't deserve to have someone love you?"

Heat rose and spread across her face. "That's not the same thing!"

Duncan didn't reply, instead just smiled. His hand had found its way back to hers, the warmth of his touch distracting her thinking process. *I have so many questions, Mother. I wish….*

"Yes."

"Yes, what?"

She took a moment to compose herself and made her decision. "I'll go back. But I won't stay."

"Of course."

"I'm just going back to talk with her. Tell her about us."

"Us?"

She stuttered as she searched for a reply. His eyes were laughing as he waited. "Us...going to Suffrom together."

"Of course."

"It doesn't mean I'll give her a second chance."

"But it's a start."

"Why do you care, anyway?"

"I may still be learning about this One True God, but I know He believes a lot in forgiveness. I believe it is His will that you forgive your mother, that He wants to restore your relationship."

"Well, I don't know if God has anything to do with it..." she muttered. Duncan raised an eyebrow at her. *I guess I did ask. Walked right into that one.* "But maybe you're right. I said I'd keep an open mind about all the God stuff." She shrugged. "Just don't get your hopes up."

Chapter Twenty

The morning that the group departed from the village was sunny, but surprisingly cold. The crisp fall wind blew through the forest as the horses moved quietly, crunching the fallen leaves with each step. A solemn mood pervaded the entire group, primarily resting on Sophia.

She had insisted on visiting Jacob's wife and son before leaving, so the night before she had knocked on their door.

"Go away!" an angry reply came from behind the closed door. "I know who you are, and I have no interest in talking to you."

Nervously, Sophia knocked again, more hesitantly this time.

"I said go away!"

Lily had warned her that Jacob's young wife might not be interested in speaking with her. She had been practically inconsolable when told of her husband's death. Now, Sophia could hear the sound of a crying baby coming from behind the door as well. She heard things being thrown, and the crying rose in volume.

I have to try. She deserves to hear the truth from me. So, she built up her courage and knocked for a third time.

The wooden door flung open with such force that Sophia thought it might come off its hinges. A young woman with flushed face and sunken eyes stood before her, holding a crying child who struggled weakly in her tight grip. "I said go away. What part of that did you not understand?"

"I wanted to tell you that…"

"That my husband is dead because of you? That I'm a widow with a son I can't provide for, who will never know his father? That my suffering is completely and utterly your fault?"

The torrent of angry words flew out and stabbed her in the heart like spears. With each hit her resolve weakened, but Sophia still pressed on, slightly regretting her decision to come alone. "I'm sorry for what happened, but…"

"You're sorry? Will sorry bring my husband back? Will sorry feed my son?"

"I…" Sophia stuttered, trying to finish a thought before being interrupted. "I wanted you to know that your husband died saving my life."

"And what does that matter? He died. It doesn't matter how."

"I thought…"

"Well you thought wrong," the woman said, stepping forward outside the doorway, causing Sophia to take a few startled steps backward. A slight twinge in her side accompanied each step. "My husband died saving you? You might as well have driven the sword through him yourself. You think I care about your life? All I know is that you're alive, and my husband is dead."

With that she slammed the door shut, leaving Sophia standing alone in the street listening to the sound of a woman sobbing and a baby screaming behind a closed door.

"Sophia?"

Her brother's voice startled her out of her memories, and she glanced to see he had ridden up on her right while she'd been reminiscing. Somehow he looked older, though that seemed impossible since she had only been gone a few months. He sat a little taller in the saddle, and he seemed more sure of himself then when she'd knocked him down in the castle corridor all those months ago. "Sorry, Solomon, I didn't hear you ride up."

"You seemed pretty lost in your thoughts there, Sis."

"I was." She didn't know what else to say.

"I'm glad you're coming home."

She nodded.

"Mother and Father were really worried about you."

"Not you?" she halfheartedly teased.

"Of course I was," he replied indignantly. "You're my sister! Why wouldn't I be worried about you?"

"I don't know. Just ignore me," she said with a sigh. "I'm not really thinking straight right now."

They rode in silence for a few minutes. "I'm sorry," Solomon said quietly. "About what happened with…you know."

"It wasn't your fault. You weren't even there."

"Still," he said, looking at her with sad eyes. "I'm sorry you had to go through all that."

"Thanks," she said, barely loud enough to be heard over the gust of wind that whipped through the forest.

Fall is a strange time for travelers. It fluctuates between the bitter cold of winter, minus the snow, and the rainy darkness of spring. On the cold days the group pressed onward, wrapping themselves with the blankets Michael and Katherine had thought to bring from the castle. On the rainy days it was harder, as the water soaked through the blankets and chilled them to the bone.

Sophia's thoughts were as dark as the weather, replaying her conversation with Jacob, the ensuing fight with his father, and a slammed door with the muffled sounds of a crying child. Prayers were difficult to come by, as she felt the weight of her decisions strangling her from the inside out. Any attempts by her traveling companions to lift her spirits fell by the wayside as she withdrew further and further into herself.

Even Helen, consumed with her own misgivings about seeing her mother again, attempted in vain to draw her quiet cousin out of her thoughts. She was met with stony silence or dismissive remarks. Katherine was more often than not found riding at her daughter's side, ready to listen should she need to speak; but more often than not simply riding in silence.

And so, the weeks went by as the group grew closer and closer to the castle.

"Are you getting excited?"

"For what?"

"To finally be home! Her Majesty thinks that we should arrive either this evening or tomorrow morning." Phillip gave her an encouraging smile, hoping to emulate the expected emotion.

A noncommittal shrug was his response. Sophia was convinced the group must be taking shifts to try and cheer her up. Earlier this morning had been her brother's turn again; she'd tried to follow his stories and smile when she was expected to laugh, but even he had grown discouraged and ridden in silence for the remainder of the morning. Surprisingly, Phillip and Solomon had struck up a sort of friendship during their travels. She'd often see them riding side by side, laughing at one another, and sharing worried looks over her continued depression. When the group had stopped for lunch, she'd seen them in deep discussion, presumably about her.

I don't mean to be so rude to him, but can't he understand I just want to be left alone?

"Well?"

"Well, what?"

"Are you getting excited?" His eyes brightened, and she lost herself for a moment in pondering them.

"Not really," she finally acquiesced.

His smile fell. "Why not? You've spoken of almost nothing else since I've met you. Now we're finally almost there, and you seem to no longer care."

"I'm not the same person as I was then."

"What do you mean?"

She stared sullenly at the reins she held loosely in her hands.

"Sophia?"

She whispered something under her breath that he didn't catch.

"Sophia," he said again, softer this time, with such gentleness that it brought tears to her eyes. "Please tell me what's wrong."

It wasn't a command, but a request. An invitation to share her pain, and after so many days of punishing herself for the weight she carried...she wanted something to ease her burden. "I'm a murderer."

"Sophia, you know that isn't true..."

"But it is," she quietly insisted, "I could have saved him, but I pushed him away from me and over the cliff instead. I was afraid and angry, and I wasn't thinking clearly…"

"He would have killed you."

"That doesn't make it right."

"He killed Jacob."

"And that's my fault too," she said, her voice choking on the tears she'd been trying so hard to hold back. "His widow was right; I may as well have driven the sword through him myself."

"Jacob wouldn't see it that way…"

"Jacob is dead," she said vehemently. She cast her angry eyes at him, filled to the brim with tears but still stubbornly refusing to spill over. "What you think he would say doesn't matter anymore…nothing matters anymore." The final words were again muttered so softly that Phillip didn't catch them; but before he could address the issue a cry went up from the front of the group.

They had arrived at the castle.

Eli remembered a day, so long ago and yet it felt like yesterday, where he found himself in the same position as now. He had spent his morning in the old familiar prayer room, pouring out his heart to the One True God. Although he loved the chapel Michael had built, that room would always hold a special place in his heart.

And now he stood on the balcony, watching the road and waiting for the return of his queen. *I hope they return before winter is upon us.* Michael and Katherine had insisted they wouldn't be gone long, convinced that they could find the girls and bring them back quickly. He hoped they were right.

How will I tell them? His heart felt so heavy as he thought of the message he must deliver upon their return. *Dear God, give me the words to say; because I fear I am at a loss.* Eli sighed, and turned away from his vigil to roam the castle halls once more.

It was then that he heard it…the happy cheers of an approaching group of travelers.

Katherine sighed as the flags flying above the castle came into view. Solomon had just flown past her on his mount, laughing as he tried to be the first to reach the gates. She felt relieved to be home, but she could not shake the heaviness in her spirit.

"Katherine?"

She met her husband's eyes with a weary smile. "Yes, Michael?"

"Happy to be home?"

"Of course," she glanced backward before she could catch herself. "I just wish everyone felt the same.

Sophia was still riding alongside Phillip, currently they seemed to be silently ignoring each other. Hanging at the furthest reaches in the back was Helen alongside Duncan, also seemingly riding in silence. The weight that hung between the young people was heavy enough to crush anyone's joy.

"Katherine?"

Her thoughts returned to Michael. "I'm sorry. I'm just worried about them. It'll be better for everyone being home I think."

He smiled. Those brown eyes still sent shivers up her spine whenever he looked at her. She was so grateful God had given her this man; and she hoped that Sophia and Solomon would be as blessed one day. *Perhaps sooner than I would've preferred,* she thought to herself as she remembered the young men riding in their company.

"They'll be fine," he assured her. "Healing takes time; but it does come eventually. Especially when you're surrounded by people who love you."

She laughed as she saw his quick fatherly glance in Phillip's direction. "Perhaps sooner than either of us would've preferred," she said quietly to herself.

Solomon, by this time, had reached the gate and was dismounting, handing his reigns off to a stable boy. Eli was standing at the gate, and the two embraced in a quick hug. Katherine and Michael were soon approaching as well, with the rest of the group filing in behind them.

"Much more decorum than your last return home, Your Majesty," Eli said with a smile that didn't quite reach his eyes.

A quick blush flooded her cheeks as she remembered the events he was talking about. "Yes, Eli, although we did bring with us a few extra guests this time as well. No new husbands though," she added as a quick clarification as Eli's eyes drifted to their gentlemen escorts.

She was still distracted by the solemn look in Eli's eyes. "Is everything well, Eli? Hopefully nothing too difficult happened in our absence."

The old man looked to the ground and didn't answer.

Michael dismounted, quickly followed by his wife. "Eli," he asked earnestly, "did something happen?"

"Your Majesties, I..." He cleared his throat to shove aside the tears. "I have a letter."

"A letter?" Katherine said puzzled.

"A letter for Helen."

The rest of the group had already handed off their horses to the stable hands who had come running when they saw the King and Queen's entourage arrive. Helen was still standing mostly apart from the group, but she perked up when she heard her name mentioned. "A letter for me? Who is it from?"

Eli pulled a folded letter from his pocket and walked slowly towards her. Hesitant to meet her eyes, he handed her the letter and then took a step back. Helen took note of the seal before opening it. "This is my mother's seal. Why would my mother write me a letter?"

Still no response from Eli. Carefully, she broke the seal and opened the folded parchment, a sense of dread settling deep into her stomach.

To my daughter, Helen:

I hope this letter finds you soon. Perhaps Eli can send it to Suffrom for me, as I know you have no intention of darkening the castle halls here in Adven again. I cannot blame you for that. Like me, these rooms have nothing but painful memories for you.

I know that I have failed as your mother. I never forgave God for taking away your father, for taking away my reason for living. But I should have tried harder for you.

I hope that someday you get all the things I couldn't give you. I hope that you're happy in Suffrom. You deserve to be happy, Helen. You deserve to be loved.

I did love you, my daughter. I know I didn't tell you that often enough. Perhaps that's why you left. If it was, I don't blame you.

I just wanted the pain to stop. I'm sorry.

Mother

"Eli, what is this?" Helen looked up from the letter and saw that Eli had lost the battle with his tears. He still couldn't meet her gaze. Dropping the paper to the ground, she grabbed his outer cloak and pulled him closer to her. "What happened while we were gone?!" she screamed as Duncan grabbed her and pulled her away.

"I'm so sorry, Your Majesty. I tried to stop her. She wouldn't listen; she just…"

Katherine shoved her way to reach Eli, putting her arm around his shoulder to comfort him while still trying to get answers. "What happened to my sister, Eli?"

Chapter Twenty-One

Words weren't enough. They could never prepare her for walking into her mother's empty room. The door creaked as she pressed it open, and her soft footsteps were the only sound in the room. Eli hadn't removed any of her mother's things yet; and of course, her things were still thrown around the room in disarray.

She'd been sick. I don't really know for how long, but she suddenly got worse. And then she stopped eating. She refused to see anyone after the King and Queen left. I tried to reason with her; Edwin tried too. But she just gave up.

Helen walked out to the balcony where her mother's chair sat where it always was. She pulled her shawl a little closer to her as a crisp fall wind blew past her. The dead garden lay beneath her.

All she did was sit on her balcony and stare at the garden. Even as the weather grew colder, it was like she didn't even notice. She just stared out into the distance. No one could talk to her; she wouldn't listen to any of us.

She stepped back inside and sat gingerly on the bed.

She must have finally just gone to sleep and never woke up. I found that letter next to her. I'm so sorry, Helen.

"Helen?"

She jumped up, startled, as her aunt stepped into the room. "Aunt Katherine."

The Queen looked tired, and suddenly much older than she'd ever seemed before. Clearly, the news of her sister's death had come as a surprise to her too. "How are you?"

"How am I supposed to be doing? My mother is dead."

"That sounds about right."

"Pardon?"

Katherine gave her a weak smile. "You sound like me after my mother died. Same snippy attitude."

Helen rolled her eyes and sat back down on the bed with a sigh. "Is this where I get a lecture about how things are going to be okay?"

"No," the Queen said as she sat on the bed next to her niece. "This is where you get a lecture about deciding what you're going to do now."

"I shouldn't have come back. I shouldn't have let Duncan talk me into it. I should have just kept going. Then I'd be in Suffrom right now, and..."

"And you would have spent your life wondering what happened to your mother."

Helen glared at her. "I *left* her, why would I care what happened to her?"

"Then why do you care now?"

"I don't know. Maybe I don't."

"You'll have a hard time convincing me of that."

The two sat in silence for a few moments before Helen said quietly, "What do I do now, Aunt Katherine? I...I really am alone now."

"I think there's a young man downstairs who might feel differently about that."

Helen blushed. "That's not...I mean..."

Katherine placed her hand on Helen's, squeezing it gently. "It's okay. I'm happy for you. Your mother would be too."

"She told me I deserved to be happy. But," she paused before continuing. "Didn't she deserve to be happy, too?"

"Yes, she did."

"Then why did she do this? Why did she spend all those years hiding here in the dark? Why didn't she just get over it, try harder, do anything other than just giving up?" Helen had stood up and began angrily pacing around the room as she talked. "Why did she just give up?"

"Helen, I..."

"We could have been happy together!" She was crying now, great big sobs escaping between her words as she stopped pacing and collapsed on the floor. "Why did she do this?"

Katherine knelt beside her and pulled her close. Shuddering between each sob, Helen buried her face in her aunt's chest and cried until she couldn't breathe.

"I don't know, Helen. We may never know. But I know that you have a choice about where you go from here. Just like Sophia has a choice; just like everyone has a choice. How you respond to tragedy determines the type of person you will become.

When our mother died, Ralyn's choice was so different. I was the one who wanted to give up. I was mad at the gods; I was mad at our mother for leaving us. I was mad at Father who buried himself in his war to deal with his grief. But," she pulled back so that she could look Helen in the eyes, "your mother chose the opposite. She didn't give up; she put her faith in the God our mother believed in. And He gave her hope that tomorrow would be better. Eventually, she convinced me that I could have the same hope.

Helen, we may never know why your mother gave up. She knew the way out, but she chose a different path. Sometimes people do that. And it's tragic. It's wrong. And I wish you didn't have to experience this. I wish I could save you from this pain. But all I can tell you is that now you have a choice about what you do next."

Instead of responding, Helen buried her face in her aunt's chest again and continued crying, more softly this time. They stayed that way for a long time, wrapped in their shared pain and loss.

"Come on, there's something I want to show you."

Phillip followed closely behind Solomon as they walked through the courtyard. Since they'd arrived, Sophia had pretty much avoided him. Helen was of course distraught after learning of her mother's death; so Duncan was keeping close tabs on her. That left Phillip to his own devices, so he'd taken to spending most of his time with Solomon.

With a hard shove, Solomon shoved open the wooden doors to the chapel. There was no one in there today, as Eli was meeting with Michael and Katherine to discuss the details for Ralyn's funeral. The two young men walked to the front and then stood there awkwardly for a few minutes.

"Solomon, what is this?"

"It's our chapel. Where we come to pray to the One True God." He shot a look at his friend. "I know you don't believe in Him."

"No, I don't."

"That's too bad."

"Why do you say that?"

"Because you must feel pretty alone."

How would he know what I've been feeling? Ever since Duncan said he was going with Helen to Suffrom I've felt.... Phillip shifted nervously. "Yeah, I guess. Sometimes anyway. Doesn't everyone?"

"I guess. But when I feel that way, I come here. I pray. I talk to God. And then I don't feel so alone."

"Glad that works for you."

"It could work for you too."

"Look, Solomon, I appreciate the thought; but..."

With a smile, the Prince waved the words away. "I figured that's what you'd say. No worries. But you love my sister, right?"

"I didn't exactly say that..."

"It's obvious; I'm not an idiot."

"Even if I was, I know that she's not interested."

"You sure about that?"

Phillip raised an eyebrow at the younger man. "You know something I don't?"

"Nope, just an observant younger brother. I know my sister better than you."

He was getting uncomfortable with this conversation. "What does this have to do with the chapel? You said you wanted to show me something?"

"It's more like I wanted to show you and tell you something." Solomon motioned to the building around him. "I wanted to show you my favorite place in the castle, since it seems like you'll be sticking around for a while. And I wanted to tell you that this is probably where you'll find me in the future."

"What are you talking about?"

Solomon ran his hand through his hair, nervously as he continued. "When Sophia left, it was the first time I ever thought about what would happen if I became king. And it terrified me. I came here a lot to talk to God about it. That's when I realized I didn't really want to be king, even if Sophia didn't come back. That wasn't my part to play." He smiled and stood a little straighter as he continued. "I decided I wanted to help people, like Eli. I wanted to be someone who could teach other people about the One True God." A glance in Phillip's direction. "I wanted to help people like you."

A puzzled nod was all he needed to continue his story.

"So, I decided I'm going to give up my title. I want to just be a teacher, an advisor, like Eli. And I don't need to be a prince to do that."

"Why would you give that up? Couldn't you help people even more if you were a prince?"

He shook his head. "Not like I want to. There would always be things getting in the way of me just being able to help people."

"What does this have to do with me, Solomon?"

With an easy smile, he put a hand on Phillip's shoulder. "I just want you to know that when you have questions, you can come to me. If you want to marry my sister, you'll have to figure this part out first."

"I didn't say I wanted…"

Another waved dismissal of his words. "Just trust the observant younger brother on this one."

Chapter Twenty-Two

The funeral took place a few days after the return of the royal family. Of course, Ralyn had already been buried, as Eli didn't know when they would return; but they gathered together in the chapel with as many of the castle staff that wished to pay their respects. Some of them had grown up with the young Princess turned Queen and were particularly devastated at her loss. Edwin was silent throughout the service, lost in his own grief. There had been some discussion of his taking some time away from the castle once spring came again. For now, everyone was settling in for winter.

Spring would bring the departure of Helen and Duncan for Suffrom as well. No longer insistent on an immediate departure, Helen had agreed to spend the winter in the castle and have a proper send off this time. Phillip had also agreed to stay through the winter, a decision that had Solomon particularly pleased.

Dressed in a black dress and thick woolen shawl, Sophia found herself seated in between her parents as the funeral began. Solomon was helping Eli with the service, as part of his training. His announcement to abdicate his claim to throne and title had come as a surprise to her, but not to her parents. They were incredibly proud of him and had encouraged him to continue his studies with Eli in a more focused manner.

I guess that just leaves me. What do I do now?

Even being back at the castle had not driven away all her guilty feelings for what had happened. And with everyone being focused on the funeral preparations and the death of her aunt, she had all the time she wanted to mope by herself. Today was the first day she had actually been forced to be with people. Even Phillip hadn't pressed her, although she assumed he would in the coming days.

"We are gathered here today to remember the life of Ralyn, Princess of Adven, Queen of Suffrom, sister of Katherine, wife of Evan, and mother of Helen. Although her life ended with tragedy, we remember the people that she touched in her life. We celebrate the life that she lived, and we comfort the people who loved her. She will be missed greatly by many, myself included."

Eli paused to gather his thoughts before he continued. Sophia was relieved that she had not been asked to share anything today. She wouldn't have been able to get through it; Eli was struggling enough as it was.

"Today I wanted to take time to share stories of her life as best remembered by her family and friends. Your Majesty?"

Queen Katherine rose and spoke for a few minutes about her sister as they were children, about the fun and laughter they shared and about the faith that got them through difficult days. There were several servants who shared similar stories. Her father and brother shared briefly, although they had far less happy times to pull from. Finally, Helen stood before the crowd, nervously clasping and unclasping her hands.

"I've been thinking a lot about my mother over these last few days. Listening to all of you talk about her, I wish I'd known her then...back when she was happy." An awkward pause as she tried to stop fidgeting. "When I think of my mother, most of what I remember is anything but happy. I grew up hating this place and everything it represented. I didn't understand why mother would stay here if she hated it so much. I mean, I guess in the end she didn't..." Helen grimaced and started shifting nervously again. "I'm sorry, that was tasteless. You'd think studying to be a queen your whole life would make you a better public speaker." She blushed and then shook her head violently as a snicker rippled through the crowd. "That wasn't what I meant to say either!"

She sighed. "What I want to say is this. Aunt Katherine told me I needed to make a decision about how I was going to respond to my mother's death. And that decision would be important because it would determine what type of person I would become. And the more I thought about that, the more I thought about how my mother responded to the death of my father. How she just kind of wasted away all those years and stopped being the happy person all of you knew. How in the end she gave up on everything: on me, on God, and ultimately her life.

And I made a decision. I decided I don't want to be like my mother, at least not how she ended. I want to be happy. I want to be loved. I want to make other people happy and love other people. And the more I thought about that, the more I thought about God and what part He might have in that decision. I think my mother was wrong to blame God for all her problems. Maybe part of it was His fault; I guess I don't really know. But I do know that when she gave up on her faith, she gave up on joy. So, I decided I wanted to try something different; I decided I wanted to give God a chance. I wanted to see if He could give me the joy I'd been searching for. So far it seems like He brought me everything else I could have wanted: family and friends who love me, who could teach me about Him.

So, that's all I wanted to say, I guess." Unsure of what to do, Helen remained standing in front of the crowd waiting for direction. Katherine rose from her seat and pressed Helen into a hug as the crowd applauded.

Sophia sat silently and thought about her cousin's words.

The weather grew colder and colder each day, with fewer leaves falling from the barren branches surrounding the castle. Sophia found herself walking the paths weaving through the dead garden, shivering slightly when the wind whipped by. She was thinking about a lot of things today. Her aunt, her cousin, her mother and father, Solomon, Phillip. And of course, Jacob. Always Jacob. The nightmares were at least starting to come less frequently. She didn't picture his father falling backward into the river every second her eyes were closed. The sounds of slamming doors and crying babies didn't darken every waking moment.

She'd stopped carrying her sword. Her mother wouldn't take it back, so right now it was locked in a trunk in her room. She didn't know if she would ever find the courage to carry it again. Every time she touched it, she felt the cold steel on her hands, so different from the warmth she'd felt while fighting. Now it felt as cold as her broken spirit.

God, you're still there, right? You haven't left me, have you?

She kept hearing Helen's words over and over. Deciding to give God a chance. Deciding that she didn't want to follow in her mother's footsteps.

God, I want to choose you too. But I just don't know how.

"Sophia?"

Her mother's voice carried softly across the deserted pathways to her ears. She looked up to see her mother, wearing a dark blue dress and a black shawl, a sharp contrast to her light blond hair. *She looks so much older than when I left.* Her eyes were weary, but a slight smile was apparent as she came closer.

"I'm surprised to find you here. It's getting colder every day. Some of the servants are whispering about snowflakes they saw this morning. Why don't you come back inside and get warm?"

"Mother?"

"Yes?"

"Will it ever stop hurting?"

"I can't promise that, Sophia."

She wrapped her arms around herself, trying to force the warmth back into her body as she tugged her shawl even closer. "I just want it to stop hurting."

Her mother remained quiet for a few minutes. Waiting.

"Mother?"

"Yes?"

"I'm going to be okay, right?"

"Yes, you are. It will take time. But yes, I believe you will be just fine."

Sophia let her hands drop back to her sides with a sigh. "I guess I just need to keep hearing that."

"You don't need to hear it from me. I think you know that."

She turned to her mother, confused.

Katherine took her daughter's hand. It felt warm against her cold skin. "I can hold your hand. I can be right here with you. I can tell you everything will be okay someday. But there's another voice you need to hear right now. I believe you've heard it before?"

"You're talking about the One True God."

"Yes, I am."

"I've been talking to Him. But He doesn't seem to answer me back."

"He will. Just be patient."

She gave her daughter a quick hug with the reminder that dinner would be served soon. Sophia remained standing in the garden for a few minutes after her mother went inside the castle.

"Are you there, God?"

There wasn't an audible response. She still stood alone surrounded by dead flowers and bushes. She still felt guilty for what had happened. She still felt sad about her aunt's death.

But she didn't feel so cold. A little flutter of warmth came to life somewhere deep inside her. A feeling that things really would get better, that they wouldn't always be this way. Hope that she could choose a better path in the future, that she could be happy again. *Maybe even be happy with Phillip*, she thought to herself with a smile.

As she turned to go inside to dinner, she paused outside the doors to the hall. She could hear her brother's laughter mixed with Phillip's. Helen was complaining about something…I guess giving God a chance didn't automatically fix someone's personality. Duncan's quiet voice could be heard in the background, perhaps trying to talk her down. Katherine and Michael's voices could be heard in the mix too, and although she couldn't understand their words, she could hear the laughter they were trying to suppress.

I choose this, God. I choose to find joy in reality.

And she opened the door.

The End